diamonds are a thief's best friend

by Hope McLean

Scholastic Inc.

With sincere thanks to editor Grace Kendall,
who has Lili's creativity, Erin's sense of humor,
Willow's energy, and Jasmine's sparkle.

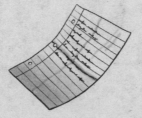

ISBN 978-0-545-60763-6

12 11 10 9 8 7 6 5 4 3 2 1   13 14 15 16 17/0

Printed in the U.S.A.   40
This edition first printing, August 2013
Previously published as *Jewel Thieves: Diamonds Are a Thief's Best Friend*
Book design by Natalie C. Sousa

Chapter One

"I can't wait to see what Lili made for the art show!" Jasmine Johnson said as she walked up the front steps of Martha Washington School. "She wouldn't let me see what she was working on."

"Probably something *fabulous*!" guessed her friend Erin Fischer with a grin. "And if I know Lili, there will be gallons of glitter involved."

Willow Albern shivered into her parka. "Remember that Christmas card she gave us? I was pulling silver glitter out of my hair for weeks!"

Willow smiled as she pushed open the school's heavy front door and a blast of warm air hit them.

"Aaaah," Jasmine sighed. "I know it's only one degree below freezing, but it feels like the South Pole out there. DC winters aren't usually this cold."

"Cool air keeps your mind sharp," Erin said. "They should hold quiz bowl outside. Then we'd get *all* the answers right!"

"We wouldn't be able to ring the buzzer if our fingers were frozen!" Jasmine argued.

Erin, Jasmine, Willow, and their friend Lili were all members of the sixth-grade Martha Washington quiz bowl team, called the Jewels. They competed against other teams, answering tough, rapid-fire questions in all subjects, including science, math, history, and art. Even though it was only their first year competing together as a team, they were doing really well. In fact, they had won enough matches to qualify for the regional tournament. Next week, they were traveling to New York City to compete!

The girls walked down the hallway to the school's art room. The building was crowded with teachers, students, and family members who had come to see the show. But not all the kids were from Martha Washington.

"It's too bad Atkinson students were invited to be in the art show," Erin said to her friends in a loud whisper. "Especially *Isabel*. But I'd face a room full of Isabels to show my support for Lili!"

What had started out as an academic rivalry between the Jewels and a competing quiz bowl team, the Atkinson Preparatory School Rivals, became personal after a daring theft in the fall. The Rivals had stolen the ruby necklace that had once belonged to Martha Washington herself from the Jewels' middle school library! As the

Rivals' history expert, Isabel Baudin was probably Erin's least favorite person.

"Well, don't look now, but there she is," Willow said, nodding down the hallway toward a girl with short blond hair.

Jasmine grabbed Willow and Erin by the arms and pulled them into the nearest empty hallway.

"Guys, I don't think I can do this!" she said dramatically. "I mean, I knew the Rivals were going to be here. But actually seeing them . . . It's so embarrassing!"

"Yeah," Erin agreed. "But so what if we had to make that ridiculous apology to the Rivals? We know the truth. They stole the Martha Washington ruby. And they are going to be sorry they ever tried to humiliate us!"

Willow's dark brown eyes flashed. "*They* should be the ones embarrassed to face *us*. We have nothing to be ashamed of."

Jasmine sighed. "I know. It's just tough, that's all."

The whole incident had been harder on Jasmine than any of the other Jewels, because she had been a suspect when the ruby was first stolen. Then when the Jewels discovered that it was, in fact, the Rivals who had stolen the ruby, the tables were turned on them. The Rivals accused the Jewels of making up the story, and the girls had to write them a formal apology. Jasmine had been really embarrassed by the whole thing. But having friends like Willow, Erin, and Lili had helped her get through it.

"Come on," Willow said, motioning to Jasmine. "Lili's waiting for us."

Erin and Jasmine followed Willow down the hall to the art room and hung up their jackets. Usually a messy space filled with tables and unfinished canvases, the art room had been transformed for the show. The tables had been moved out, making the room seem much bigger. And white lights had been strung around the ceiling to enhance the finished pieces that hung from the walls. Standing easels with paintings on display dotted the middle of the room. Student artists stood close to their work, ready to discuss it with anyone who came by. Friends and family members meandered through the crowded show, admiring the art.

Willow did a quick scan of the room. "Rivals to the right," she whispered to her friends, with a nod toward a group of sixth graders.

"Oh, great. It's the Not-So-Fantastic Four," Erin muttered.

Isabel Baudin's stylish hair was held back with a sparkly headband. She was laughing as she spoke with Aaron Santiago, the team's art specialist. He stood in front of his own self-portrait. Willow grudgingly admitted to herself that it was good. He had captured his own brown eyes, dark hair, and handsome face perfectly in the oil painting.

Veronica Manasas, a science whiz, listened to their conversation. She had her long, dark hair pulled into a messy ponytail. A tall boy with wavy blond hair stood next to her. Ryan Atkinson was their team captain and math master. He was the only one of the Rivals to notice the Jewels' entrance. His eyes met Willow's and he gave that mocking little smile she had come to hate. It made her want to use her years of martial arts training to show Ryan what she was really made of.

Beside her, Erin scowled and Jasmine visibly tensed up. Willow took a deep breath to calm down. If the Jewels were going to beat the Rivals at quiz bowl and foil whatever other jewel-heist plans they had, she couldn't let them get under her skin.

"Hey, there's Lili!" Willow shook off the negative vibes and focused on her friend, who was standing next to a painting on the wall on the opposite side of the room.

"Lili!" Erin yelled. She ran through the crowd and flung herself at her friend.

Lili squealed with delight and hugged Erin close.

"I'm so glad to see you guys!" she said happily as she looked up at Willow and Jasmine. "The show is going fantastic!"

"Lili, this is so amazing!" Jasmine said as she gazed at her friend's self-portrait. "I love it!"

In the colorful painting, an animated version of Lili flew through the starry night sky. It was creative, funky, and fun, just like Lili herself.

"It's my take on Van Gogh's *Starry Night*," she explained. "We had to create two pieces for the show. One had to be a self-portrait; the second could be anything we'd like. Can you guess what my second piece is?" She took a step back from the girls and looked at them expectantly.

Even though it was Lili's first year at Martha Washington School, the Jewels knew her well. Their artistic friend loved to express herself through her clothes and hairstyles. Tonight, her glossy black hair was devoid of any of the strands of color or decoration that usually adorned it. She wore what appeared to be a simple black dress, but she had used silver ink and hand-stitched beads and stars to recreate Van Gogh's *Starry Night* on the front.

"Wow," Willow said. "It's beautiful."

Lili beamed. "Thanks! I worked really hard on it." Then she nodded to Willow. "Ooh, I totally love your shirt!"

Willow wore a long-sleeved baseball tee. But instead of a team name written across the front, it said MATHLETE.

"It's true. She's the Jewels' math MVP!" Erin chimed in.

Lili laughed. "I'm so thirsty! I've been talking about my art all night," she said. "Not that I don't love that! But I need a drink. Let's go to the classroom next door. They're serving refreshments in there. My mom and grandma volunteered to help out."

"Yum! I hope your mom made those chocolate fudge cupcakes I love so much." Erin was practically drooling.

"Where is Eli?" Willow asked about Lili's brother, a high school student at Atkinson Prep.

Lili rolled her eyes. "Computer Club meeting. They're, like, building a supercomputer or something."

The girls were making their way through the crowded room toward the door when Isabel stepped in front of them, blocking their path.

"Hello there," she said in her lilting French accent. "I wanted to let you know I have decided to accept your little apology." She smirked.

Erin's face turned redder than her auburn hair. Her freckles looked like they were going to jump right off her face. "You — you," she stuttered, "you . . ."

"Do you need to go outside and get some air?" Isabel asked Erin innocently. "You look very hot."

"I'm fine!" Erin managed. "They've just got the heat cranked way up in here, that's all."

Isabel gave a high, tinkling laugh before walking away.

"We better get a cupcake into her, and quick." Jasmine gestured at Erin.

Erin wasn't even paying attention. "The nerve of her!"

Lili grabbed Erin's hand. "Cupcakes, think of cupcakes," she said soothingly as she led her out of the room.

Parents and students milled about, enjoying their refreshments, in the next classroom. Lili's mom, Mrs. Higashida, and grandma, Mrs. Takahashi, stood behind a table loaded with cookies, cupcakes, drinks, and other treats.

Lili dragged Erin over to the table. "One chocolate cupcake, stat, please!"

Mrs. Higashida laughed. "Is Erin having another cupcake emergency?" She placed one of the fudgy cakes on a paper plate and handed it to Erin. "Here you go. Enjoy!"

Erin took a huge bite. "Delicious," she mumbled with her mouth full. Chocolate frosting was smeared across her lips.

Lili reached for a soda, but her grandmother called out sharply, "Lili! Soda on top of a cupcake is way too much sugar."

Lili sighed. "Okay, Obaasan, I'll have some water instead."

Mrs. Higashida smiled at the girls. "What do you think of the art show?" she asked.

"We've only really seen Lili's work so far, but we're impressed," Jasmine said. "It is so cool to have such a talented friend."

"Yes, I am very impressed as well," Principal Frederickson joined in. She had walked over to the table while the girls were talking. "With all our students. And especially you, Lili. Great work."

Principal Frederickson was an older woman, and she always looked put-together and professional. Not a curled dark hair was ever out of place. Even though she could be pretty scary, the Jewels had turned to her for help when the Rivals had stolen the ruby.

"Um, thanks!" Lili said. The principal usually made her a little nervous.

"And good luck at the regional meet next weekend," Principal Frederickson said. "I know that it's been a stressful few months for you girls. But we are proud to have you representing Martha Washington in this competition."

"Thank you," Willow replied. "We'll do you — and the school — proud."

Principal Frederickson nodded slightly and looked like she was moving on when Erin spoke up.

"Principal Frederickson, we were wondering something," she said. "You used to go to this school, right?"

"Well, yes, I did. A long time ago," their principal replied with a quizzical look. "Why do you ask, Erin?"

"Well, did you ever hear a rumor about the Martha Washington ruby being part of a group of gems? Like, four jewels together?"

Their principal looked startled, but quickly regained her composure. "The ruby again? I thought you girls were done with that." The tone of her voice clearly said that she thought they *should* be done with it. "Of course we miss having that beautiful necklace on campus, but the police did their best. It's gone."

"We *are* done with it," Jasmine said quickly. "Sorry to bother you."

Principal Frederickson nodded again and walked away without another word.

"Why did you ask that?" Jasmine hissed at Erin.

Erin shrugged. "I thought she might know something, since she went to Martha Washington herself. That letter I found from Martha

Washington said there were three other jewels, and they're all important somehow, remember?"

"Yes, of course I remember, but we need to be thinking about the tournament right now, not jewels," Willow reminded her. As team captain, she was always keeping them on track.

"I'm definitely thinking about the tournament," Erin promised. "That's where I'll wipe that smile off of Isabel's face. We've got to beat the Rivals!"

Willow nodded. "New York is our chance to rebuild our quiz bowl reputation."

"We know," Jasmine reminded her. "That's why we've been studying like crazy! I've been brushing up on everything and anything science."

"And I've been so into history, it's like I built a time machine," Erin said. "Even my dreams are historical! Last night, I dreamt I was riding alongside Paul Revere. But instead of yelling 'The British are coming!' I was crying 'The Rivals are coming!'"

Lili laughed at that before her face turned serious. "I need to get cracking," she admitted. "I've been so busy getting ready for this show, I slacked off on studying art history."

"We've got a bunch of practices scheduled this week," Willow assured her. "We'll be ready."

"I hope so." Lili nodded. "Oh, and thanks for agreeing to stay after the show and help clean up."

"No problem," Jasmine said. "Speaking of the show, let's see the rest of it."

The girls spent the remainder of the night looking at art and chatting with some of their other friends from school. Thankfully, there were no more run-ins with any of the Rivals.

The crowds cleared out and the girls stayed behind to help Mrs. Higashida and Mrs. Takahashi clean up. Erin pushed a broom around the refreshments room.

"I think most of those crumbs are yours." Willow laughed.

Erin grinned. "Pretty likely."

"Thanks again, girls," Mrs. Higashida said after they were done. "Ready to go? I'll bring the van around to the front."

While Lili's mom and grandmother walked to the parking lot, the girls put on their jackets. Lili's, as always, stood out. This time it was a bright teal sweater coat with crocheted multicolored sleeves she had sewn on.

As she slipped her hands into the pockets, Lili felt something odd.

"What's this?" she said as she pulled out a folded piece of yellow lined notebook paper. Lili unfolded the paper and read it, then gasped.

"What does it say?" Willow asked.

Lili read the note out loud. "It says 'Forget about the ruby. It's the diamond you need to worry about now. Watch the Rivals in NYC. It's up to you to keep the diamond safe and out of their hands.'"

Jasmine's green eyes narrowed. "It sounds like the Rivals are planning to strike again."

Willow nodded. "And this time, we're going to stop them!"

Chapter Two

The next day the Jewels walked through the crowded food court of the Hallytown Mall. They had spent the morning shopping for their trip to New York, and now they were hungry.

"Here's an empty table!" Erin called.

The girls hurried over, balancing shopping bags and food trays.

"Whew!" Lili said as she slid into a chair. "That feels good. My feet hurt."

"Hey, you're the one who wanted to shop till you dropped," Willow reminded her. "And I thought we were supposed to practice for quiz bowl today?"

Jasmine nodded. "We'll have to study when we get back to your house, Willow. But the mall was a good idea. I did need a few things for our trip to the Big Apple."

She reached into her bag and pulled out a fuzzy purple beret. Then she put it on top of her curly brown hair and struck a pose.

"What do you think?" she asked.

"It's warm — *and* stylish," Lili said. "Love it!"

Willow dug her fork into her grilled chicken salad, while Lili started making her way through a huge plate of cheese fries.

"So, about that note Lili got last night," Willow said between bites. "Anyone have any ideas?"

Erin nodded as she swallowed a forkful of spicy chicken gumbo. "I'm trying to connect the dots. First, the Rivals steal the Martha Washington ruby. Second, we find a letter from Martha Washington to someone named Abigail — probably Abigail Adams — about four jewels: a ruby, diamond, emerald, and sapphire. Martha tells Abigail she has hidden the jewels and is worried about someone finding them and putting them all together. Third, Lili gets a mysterious note telling her to keep the diamond out of the Rivals' hands."

Erin leaned back in her chair and folded her arms over her stomach. "Coincidence?" she asked as she arched her eyebrow. "I think not. The diamond the Rivals are after must be the one from Martha's letter!"

Jasmine frowned. "I'm not sure. It's confusing. How do we know they've even seen the letter?"

"We don't," Willow agreed. "But I think this note proves that they've found out about the four jewels somehow. Why else would they be after the diamond now?"

"Right," Erin agreed, nodding. "I mean, at first, I thought they stole the ruby for money. Or maybe just to hurt Martha Washington School in some way. But if they want the diamond, it means they must know about the four jewels. Martha said that the four jewels had to be together. I bet the Rivals are trying to get all four of them."

Jasmine looked thoughtful. "Okay. So maybe they have the sapphire and the emerald, or maybe they don't. But if that note is right, then they definitely don't have the diamond."

"That's good, right?" Lili asked, stabbing another clump of cheese fries with her fork. "That means we can try to find it first?"

"How are we supposed to do that?" Willow wondered. "New York is a big city! There must be thousands of diamonds there, and we don't even know what this one looks like."

The girls were silent for a moment as this sunk in. The din of the crowded mall echoed through the food court.

Lili sat up. "I bet the person who slipped the note into my pocket knows! I wish we could ask them."

"It had to be someone who was at the art show," Willow pointed out.

Erin groaned. "Great! So that narrows it down to about a hundred students, two hundred parents, fifty teachers, Principal Frederickson, and Lili's grandma."

Lili laughed. "I always suspected she was leading a secret life. She's almost never home." All the girls giggled.

"It could be anyone, or any*thing*. For all we know, an alien could have left us that note," Erin joked.

But Jasmine looked worried. "What if this is some kind of prank? What if the Rivals are just trying to make us look stupid again?"

The girls grew quiet as everyone thought that over. When the Jewels had first suspected that the Rivals stole the ruby, they had told Principal Frederickson. She told the director of Atkinson Prep, Arthur Atkinson. And then he had gone on the news and accused the girls of making false accusations! It had been an awful ordeal.

"I wouldn't put it past them," Willow said thoughtfully. "But we can't ignore this letter. We've got to investigate."

"Fine," Jasmine said. "Let's just do it *quietly*, okay?"

Erin nodded to Willow. "Okay, Nancy Drew. I've got some info for you. I did some research last night, and Martha and George Washington spent time in New York City, in a building called Federal Hall. It was the first Capitol Building of the United States, and George gave his first inauguration speech from the balcony."

Lili got excited, almost knocking over her fries. "Martha could have hidden the diamond there!"

"Maybe, but here's the bad news. Federal Hall was demolished in 1812, before being rebuilt. And Martha died in 1802, so it's not likely we'd find the diamond there." Erin explained.

"I learned something that might help," Jasmine jumped in. "I did a search to find out if there were any diamonds on display in New York from the Revolutionary War era, and I got a match. I found a museum with a temporary exhibit of colonial jewelry. A pair of diamond earrings from the 1700s is part of the showing."

"Maybe those are the diamonds the Rivals are after!" Lili said.

"It's a possibility," Willow agreed, then took another bite of her salad. "It's worth checking out. We'll have to play it really cool, do some more investigating and keep a close eye on the Rivals when we get to New York. We've got to make sure they don't steal the diamond, wherever it is."

Lili got a dreamy look in her eye. "I can't wait to visit the Met when we're there. I was researching things for us to do in New York, and I saw that the museum has a new exhibit with colonial furniture and art. So I double-checked their website last night, but it doesn't look like it includes jewelry."

"Sounds like the diamond earrings may be the best place to start," Willow suggested. "Do you know what museum they're in?"

"The Fraunces Tavern Museum," Jasmine said.

Erin frowned. "That sounds so familiar. I seem to remember something about that, but it's just dancing around in my brain and I can't catch it!"

"While Erin's thinking, we should —" Willow began, but Erin interrupted her with a loud "Aha!"

"I got it!" She leapt to her feet, knocking over her chair. "The Fraunces Tavern is where George Washington gave his farewell address to the officers of the Continental Army!"

Everyone looked at her. Erin blushed as she grabbed the chair off the floor. "I'm sorry, but I told you I've been studying like crazy for quiz bowl. And since finding that letter from Martha, I've been reading a lot about the American Revolution."

"It's okay." Lili smiled. "If you weren't history-obsessed, you wouldn't be Erin!"

"Thanks," Erin said with a grin. "That reminds me. I requested a bunch more books about Martha Washington from the school library. Did you know they have a whole section dedicated to her? Anyway, when I got home and took them out of my backpack, there was a book in my stack that I don't remember checking out. But it's really cool."

"What was it?" Jasmine asked.

"It looks like a diary," Erin replied. "Actually, it looks like it might be Martha Washington's diary. I must have grabbed it by mistake."

Jasmine looked worried. "That sounds pretty important, Erin. Maybe it's supposed to stay in the library."

Erin shrugged. "Maybe. But I want to check it out first. I got through the first thirty pages, but I haven't found anything about the jewels yet. I'm going to keep looking, though."

Willow pulled out her phone to check the time.

"We should start making our way back to the multiplex," she said. "The movie will be over soon, and I don't want to keep my mom and brothers waiting."

Willow's mom, Mrs. Albern, had given them a ride to the mall. She had taken Willow's three younger brothers, Jason, Michael, and Alex, to see a movie while the girls shopped.

They gathered up their shopping bags and trays, threw their trash in the garbage, and made their way out of the food court.

"Can we stop for ice cream on the way over?" Erin asked. "That Ragin' Cajun cuisine left my mouth burning!"

"We've got time," Willow said. "I could go for a fro-yo myself."

As the girls approached the ice cream kiosk, Erin stopped in her tracks.

"What have I done to deserve this?" she asked dramatically. "It's like stepping in gum. No matter what you do, you can't get it all off your shoe."

Standing on the line for ice cream was Isabel. She stood next to a few other girls from Atkinson, laughing and chatting. Anyone looking at her would think she was an ordinary sixth-grade girl, not a jewel thief. But the Jewels knew better.

"I hate to admit it, but she *is* stylish," Lili said. "I love that outfit!"

Isabel wore a pair of brilliant blue skinny jeans, zebra ballet flats, and a long black cami embellished with sparkling rhinestones.

Erin flashed Lili a dirty look.

"I can't help the truth!" Lili cried. "I guess I'm just used to seeing her in the Atkinson uniform."

"Whatever! She's not stopping me from getting ice cream," Erin said as she marched over to the line.

Jasmine looked at Willow and Lili, shrugged, and followed Erin. Isabel spotted them walking over. She stopped her conversation and rolled her green eyes.

"I guess they'll let *anybody* into this place," she said loudly.

Erin flashed her an evil grin. "I guess so, if *you're* here," she replied.

Isabel waved her hand dismissively in the air. "It doesn't matter. You can say whatever you want. But we will still win at quiz bowl."

"Is that so?" Erin asked, her hands on her hips. "Well, guess what? I can beat you at anything. Name it. Spelling bee? I'll take it.

Monopoly? I'm the winner. Hot-dog-eating contest? I'll leave you in the dust!"

Isabel looked at Erin like she was crazy, then exchanged glances with her friends. "She seriously needs help."

Jasmine started shaking as she tried to hold in her laughter. Willow saw that Erin was ready to go off on Isabel again, so she jumped in.

"Hey, Isabel?" she asked innocently. "Do you and the Rivals have any other plans in New York?"

Isabel seemed startled. A look of concern flashed over her face, but she quickly concealed it.

"The usual." She shrugged. "Come on," she said to her friends, "let's go."

As Isabel and her pals walked off, Jasmine and Lili exploded into laughter.

"A hot-dog-eating contest?" Jasmine said between breaths.

"Monopoly? A spelling bee?" Lili could barely get the words out, she was laughing so hard. "Erin, where do you come up with this stuff?"

"I don't know." Erin's face was bright red. "It's like, as soon as I see her, I get so mad my brain short-circuits or something!"

While her friends were laughing, Willow looked serious. "Did any of you notice Isabel's face when I asked her what their plans were for New York?"

"Now that you mention it, she did look kind of worried," Jasmine said.

"I think Isabel just slipped up and confirmed that our mystery note is right on," Willow pointed out. "The Rivals definitely have something planned for New York, and it's not only trying to win quiz bowl."

"We'll stop them," Erin said confidently. "Look out New York, here come the Jewels!"

Chapter Three

"I can't believe we'll be in New York City in only two hours and fifty-six minutes!" Willow said, gazing out the train window.

Next to her, Jasmine laughed. "Willow, are you going to keep announcing the time every five minutes?"

"I can't help it," Willow replied. "I've never been before. And there's so much I want to see!"

She turned around and looked over the top of her blue seat to talk to Ms. Keatley, who sat in the row behind her. A Social Studies teacher at Martha Washington, Ms. Keatley was the official advisor to the Jewels quiz bowl team and the girls' chaperone on this trip.

"Ms. Keatley, do you think we'll have time to see the Statue of Liberty?" Willow asked.

The teacher looked up from the book she was reading. "Quite possibly," she replied. "I've put together a rough itinerary for us, but I left some free time so we can be sure to do some things you girls will enjoy."

Willow suddenly thought of their other goal for the trip — to find the Martha Washington diamond and prevent the Rivals from stealing it.

"Um, I heard that there's an interesting exhibit at the Fraunces Tavern Museum," she said, remembering what Jasmine had discovered. "That's the reason Principal Frederickson gave us an extra couple of days for this trip, right? To have educational experiences? That would be a good one."

Ms. Keatley's green eyes lit up. "That's on my list of museums I've always wanted to visit! I'd love to go. But we should ask the others."

Willow sat back down in her seat and nudged Jasmine. "Could you get Lili and Erin?" she asked.

The girls were sitting in the two seats across the aisle from Willow and Jasmine. Lili was drawing in her sketchbook, Erin was reading a guidebook of Manhattan, and both girls had their earbuds in and were listening to music. Jasmine got up and tapped Lili on the shoulder.

"What's up?" she asked, removing an earbud. Bouncy music streamed from the tiny speakers.

"Ms. Keatley wants to talk to us," Jasmine explained. "Can you poke Erin? She's totally stuck in that book."

Soon Erin and Lili were crowded into the empty seat next to Ms. Keatley, while Willow and Jasmine leaned over the backs of their own.

"We were talking about the itinerary," Ms. Keatley said. "I want to make sure we make the most of our time here. Principal Frederickson is expecting a report from us on one of the city's great museums. But we need to plan some fun things, too."

"Well that shouldn't be a problem," Erin said. "We're here for like a week, right?"

"Five days, but we've already got a busy schedule," Ms. Keatley corrected her. "Let's see. Today is Wednesday, and I thought that we could get some pizza after we check into our hotel."

"Can we go to Famous Sal's Pizza?" Erin asked. "They featured it on the Food Channel. It's supposed to be the best pizza in, like, the world."

Ms. Keatley opened her messenger bag and started rifling through a bunch of papers and books. "I'll just have to check and see if it's near our hotel."

"Five blocks south," Erin said quickly. "I already checked it out."

"Okay then," Ms. Keatley said. "Tonight we're seeing *Transformers: The Musical* on Broadway. Tomorrow afternoon there's an opening reception for the quiz bowl tournament. Then there's nothing until dinner on Friday night because of the early high school rounds.

Saturday and Sunday is the middle school tournament. And of course we'll need to get in some practice time."

Willow looked right at Erin and Lili. "I was telling Ms. Keatley that we should go to the Fraunces Tavern Museum," she said with a tone in her voice that clearly meant, "You know, the one exhibiting the diamond earrings."

"A tavern?" Lili asked. "Aren't we too young?"

Erin nudged her. "No, it's that cool museum where George Washington gave that speech."

"Oh, yeah!" Lili said. "Yeah, we definitely want to go there."

"Maybe Friday then," Ms. Keatley said, writing in her notebook.

"Ms. Keatley, are you ever going to use a smartphone like the rest of the world?" Jasmine asked.

The teacher sighed and pushed a strand of stray blond hair behind her ear. "Honestly, it's all so complicated. The technology changes every day and each new phone is more expensive than the last."

She held up her notebook. "Ninety-nine cents. You can't beat that."

Erin's stomach rumbled. "Can we finish this schedule talk later? I need a snack. I thought we passed a food car when we got on board. Anyone want to come with me?"

"I'll go," Jasmine offered. "I'm bored. I can't read on a train or I get a stomachache."

"I'm pretty sure it's this way," Erin said, pointing to the back of the train.

She and Jasmine made their way down the aisle. When they stepped into the next passenger car, Jasmine got a worried look on her face.

"Do you think the Rivals are on this train?" she asked.

"I doubt it," Erin answered. "They probably took a private jet or something. Everyone at that school is super-rich!"

"Not Eli," Jasmine pointed out.

"Okay, well most of them are," Erin said. "Anyway, the school is super-fancy so they could probably afford some other way to get there."

"Unless they're in first class," Jasmine said, looking around nervously again.

"Well, if they're in first class they won't need to come to the food car," Erin said. "Some guy in a suit will bring it to them."

"You know, I was thinking about the Rivals and the four jewels," Jasmine said. "Remember when we were at their school, and we saw that photo of the Atkinson sapphire?"

Erin nodded. "Yeah. The one that got stolen, right?"

"It just seems like too much of a coincidence," Jasmine said. "Our school had a ruby, and theirs had a sapphire. I wonder if it's the sapphire Martha Washington was talking about?"

Erin theatrically put her hands on her head. "The sapphire? I thought we were looking for a diamond!" The girls giggled. "Seriously, though, let's focus on one jewel at a time, or it'll get too confusing. There are so many possibilities." She began to talk in a robotic voice. "Brain . . . can't . . . function. Need . . . fuel."

Jasmine laughed. "Come on, here's the food car."

The train's café car looked like a diner or small restaurant right on the train. Booths lined the window side of the car, and on the other side was a long counter with stools. Men and women in business suits had taken up most of the counter to drink coffee, eat a muffin or a bagel, and busily type on their laptops.

Erin scanned the menu on the wall and approached the register.

"I'll have one snack pack, please," she said. "And a chocolate milk."

The young woman behind the register smiled at the girls. "Anything for you?" she asked Jasmine.

"One banana, please," Jasmine said.

"That'll just be a minute," the cashier told them, after she had rung them up and taken their money.

Erin turned away from the counter and faced Jasmine. "It's all so weird, isn't it?"

"What do you mean?" Jasmine asked.

"I don't know, I guess, last year in fifth grade the most exciting thing that happened was when I learned how to weave a basket at Colonial Williamsburg. This year, I'm traveling to exotic locations to answer questions and chasing jewel thieves. Big difference."

Jasmine nodded. "I know what you mean. Sometimes none of this seems real!"

"Order's up, girls!"

Erin turned around and picked up their food. Her snack pack was a small cardboard box with a chocolate milk, an apple, a packet of mixed nuts, and some cheese. Jasmine raised an eyebrow.

"An apple? I didn't know you ate . . . you know, healthy stuff," she said.

"I'm an equal opportunity eater," Erin insisted as they headed back to their train car.

"But I thought you ate French fries for breakfast," Jasmine said.

"Only once," Erin replied. "No, wait, twice. But just because I love French fries doesn't mean that I don't also love brussels sprouts."

Jasmine made a face. "Your stomach must be made of iron."

They got back to their seats, and Erin pushed past Lili, who was busy sketching again. Erin grabbed her apple out of the box and took a bite. Then she noticed a yellow, folded slip of paper peeking out from under the package of nuts.

Curious, Erin opened it up and read the note.

"No way!" she yelled, and then she quickly cupped her hand over her mouth. She leaned over Lili to see if Ms. Keatley had noticed, but the teacher was dozing in her chair.

"What is it?" Lili asked.

Erin motioned for Jasmine and Willow to come over. "Guys, quick!" she hissed. She showed them the slip of paper. "I think we got another message from our mysterious helper."

'Twas brillig, and the slithy toves did gyre and gimble in the wabe. Thursday, 1500 hours.

"So we *are* dealing with aliens," Erin said.

"Or else really bad spellers," Lili added.

"It's from a poem," Jasmine explained. "By Lewis Carroll, that guy who wrote *Alice in Wonderland*. I think it's called . . . 'Jabberwocky'!"

"But what does it mean?" Erin asked.

Jasmine shrugged. "He made up words for the poem, so it's kind of weird. But I think it's about a battle against some monster."

Lili shook her head. "It doesn't make sense!"

"The second line does," Willow said. "Fifteen hundred hours is military time for three in the afternoon. So the second line means Thursday at three o'clock."

"Like a meeting time," Jasmine guessed. "But why would someone want to meet us?"

"And where?" Lili asked.

"We're forgetting the most important question," Willow said. "*Who?*"

Chapter Four

"No way! Is this really our hotel?" Lili asked, staring up at the tall building in front of them.

"Yes way. This place is awesome!" Erin agreed.

The Park West Hotel was a tall, granite building that towered over Fifty-seventh Street. It was sandwiched between a café on the left and a store that sold fancy shoes on the right. Two evergreen bushes trimmed into perfect cone shapes sat in marble pots that flanked the gleaming glass doors.

Ms. Keatley paid the cab driver and turned to the girls. "Some of the tournament events will be held in the conference rooms here, and the final rounds will take place in a college auditorium a few blocks away."

"It's the perfect location," Jasmine enthused. "It's close to Central Park, the shops on Fifth Avenue, Times Square, Lincoln Center . . ."

"And Famous Sal's Pizza," Erin reminded her. "Can we go get lunch soon?"

"As soon as we get settled," Ms. Keatley said. "We've got to get our luggage up to our rooms."

A man in a dark red uniform and a matching red cap approached them, rolling a big metal luggage cart next to him.

"I can help you with that," he said with a grin, and the girls thanked him as he loaded their bags onto the cart and rolled it inside.

Then they followed Ms. Keatley into the lobby. While she checked in at the front desk, the girls looked around in wonder.

Polished white marble covered the floor of the main lobby, which was furnished with sleek red couches and dark wood tables. A sparkling chandelier lit up the space.

"Wow, I feel like a movie star!" Jasmine said.

Ms. Keatley took the keys from the desk clerk. "All right, girls, to the elevator."

When they got to the twenty-second floor they found their luggage waiting for them in front of their door.

"We have a suite," Ms. Keatley explained. "You girls get your own room to share, and I'll have mine."

She pushed open the door to reveal a quaint room with a small sofa, a mini-fridge, a coffee table, and a work space with two chairs. Across the room, two large windows looked out onto the city.

"Wow!" Erin said, looking around the living area.

"This room is even cleaner than my grandma's house," Lili remarked.

Willow ran into one of the bedrooms and swept her hand over the soft gray-and-white striped bedspread. The gray matched the carpet on the floor and the stripes in the curtain panels. The walls were a pale cream, and the furniture in the room was the same dark wood as the lobby.

"It's peaceful," Willow said. "A good study environment."

Jasmine walked to the bedroom window. "It's totally amazing. But I was kind of hoping we'd have a view of Central Park."

Erin flopped down on the bed. "It's huge!"

"Yay! Sleepover party!" Lili yelled. She picked up a pillow and playfully whacked Erin over the head with it.

"There will be *no* pillow fights," Ms. Keatley said firmly. "Fun, yes, but within limits. I'll be right next door, so I'll be able to hear if you're up to any shenanigans."

"Yes, Ms. Keatley," Lili and Erin said at the same time.

"How about we bring in our bags and then go out for pizza?" the teacher suggested. "I must admit that I'm very hungry myself."

Erin quickly jumped off the bed. "Yes! Let's go!"

A few minutes later they were walking down Fifth Avenue. It was at least fifteen degrees colder than in DC, so the girls wore their winter coats, hats, and gloves. But they were so excited to be in Manhattan that they didn't feel the cold at all.

Businessmen and women in dark overcoats hurried past them, while tourists in colorful parkas walked more slowly, pointing out the buildings and the sights.

"We're heading toward Times Square, aren't we?" Lili asked. "Ooh, I heard there's a Hello Kitty store there."

"Pizza first, cute Japanese kitties later," Erin said, with a hungry look.

The famous pizzeria had big glass windows looking out onto the street corner, and the girls could see customers eating lunch and chefs in white aprons tossing pizza dough behind the counter. The place was crowded, but the girls managed to squeeze into a table in the corner.

"I'll go order our pizza," Ms. Keatley offered. "What do you girls want?"

"Let's get the works!" Erin suggested. "That way there's something for everyone."

Willow, Lili, and Jasmine knew there was no use in arguing.

"Sounds good to me," said Ms. Keatley. "I'll get us some drinks, too."

As the teacher made her way up to the counter, Willow noticed four familiar faces walk through the door.

"Oh, great," she said. "Look who's here!"

It was the Rivals, accompanied by a tall man with wavy brown hair.

"That's their advisor, Josh Haverford," Willow said. "He's usually pretty hands-off, but I guess even the Rivals need a chaperone."

Mr. Haverford said something to the Rivals and went up to the counter. Then Ryan Atkinson noticed the Jewels sitting in the back and motioned for the Rivals to follow him.

"So you guys made it," he said, in a tone that was more challenging than friendly.

"Of course," Willow shot back, looking him in the eye. "We took the train this morning."

"So did we," Ryan replied. "Funny we didn't see you. Oh, that's right — it's because we were in *first* class."

Erin and Jasmine exchanged glances. Just as they had guessed! Erin rolled her eyes.

"And I guess we're in the same hotel, then, too," Jasmine said.

"Oh, yes, and it is beautiful," Isabel said. "We have such a lovely view of Central Park."

Jasmine looked at Erin again. It was so unfair! Why did everything always work out for the Rivals?

"That's nice. Sorry we got these sweet seats at Sal's first," Erin challenged. "I don't know where you guys will sit."

Aaron flashed a smile at her. "I saw on the Food Channel that it's the best pizza in the city."

"Maybe even the world," Erin corrected him, but she was clearly pleased to meet someone with the same appreciation for pizza as she had.

Ms. Keatley walked up to the table, carrying a pizza on a metal tray. The Rivals' advisor was behind her, holding five bottles of water.

"I think there's a table opening up over there, guys," he said, nodding toward the opposite corner of the room. "Why don't you go grab it?"

The Rivals obeyed, and Mr. Haverford placed the water on the table. He looked at Ms. Keatley and smiled.

"It's too bad we couldn't find a table closer to you," he said, and behind him, Erin rolled her eyes.

"Yes, it's very crowded in here," Ms. Keatley replied in her usual flustered manner. Then she returned his gaze. "Thanks for helping with the water."

"No problem," Mr. Haverford replied. "You know, I was thinking it would be nice if our teams could do something together while we're here. DC pride and all that. We've got to stick together."

"Well, the girls and I were just working up our schedule," Ms. Keatley explained. "We're not sure what we're doing yet."

Mr. Haverford looked disappointed, but he pressed on. "Well, Ryan and the other kids were asking about something going on at the Fraunces Tavern Museum. Some exhibit or something."

The girls looked at each other with wide eyes.

"Oh?" Willow asked, raising an eyebrow. "I didn't know the Rivals were interested in colonial jewelry."

"Is that what it is?" the advisor asked with a shrug. "I guess that's interesting. Anyway, it would be nice if we could all go, you know, together."

He looked right at Ms. Keatley again when he asked, but she didn't seem to notice the attention.

"Ah, yes, Fraunces Tavern," she said absently, as she passed paper plates around the table. "The girls mentioned that, too. We'll see."

"Do you have my cell phone number?" Mr. Haverford asked. "You know, so we can set things up."

"I don't think so," Ms. Keatley replied. "Yikes! I forgot the napkins."

She hurried off. Mr. Haverford frowned and headed back up to the counter.

The girls leaned into the table, excited.

"You know what this means," Willow said. "The Rivals are planning to steal the diamond from Fraunces Tavern!"

"Oh my gosh!" Jasmine exclaimed. "Our guess about the diamond was right!"

Chapter Five

Jasmine motioned for them all to be quiet as Ms. Keatley came back to the table with napkins.

"What are you girls so excited about?" she asked.

Jasmine thought quickly. "Well, Mr. Haverford was totally flirting with you. Didn't you notice?" It wasn't exactly what she was thinking, but it certainly seemed to be true.

Ms. Keatley blushed. "Honestly, Jasmine, you have quite an imagination."

"But she's right," Lili chimed in, catching on. "He kept looking at you with googly eyes and stuff."

Ms. Keatley just shook her head. "Come on, let's dig in. This looks delicious!"

Each girl put a slice of pizza on her plate. The table got quiet as everyone ate.

"Oh, man, this is awesome!" Erin said after her first bite.

"It's definitely the best pizza I've ever eaten," Jasmine agreed.

"It's the best in the *world*," Erin reminded her.

"So, what do you think of Mr. Haverford's idea?" Ms. Keatley asked. "Going to Fraunces Tavern with the Rivals?"

The girls looked at each other, and they were all thinking the same thing: If they were going to stop the Rivals, the Jewels had to get there first.

"No way," Erin said. "I don't want to go anywhere with those guys."

The other Jewels quickly caught on to Erin's strategy.

"That's right," Jasmine agreed. "Not after what happened. It's too soon."

Ms. Keatley nodded sympathetically. "I understand. But it sounds like they're trying to become friends."

"No, Mr. Haverford is trying to become *your* friend," Jasmine countered, and Ms. Keatley blushed again. The girls giggled.

"You know what I think? I think we should go right after lunch," Erin suggested.

Ms. Keatley looked startled. "So soon?"

"Why not?" Willow joined in. "We have a free afternoon, right?"

"Well, yes," the teacher answered hesitantly. She wiped her hands on a napkin and dug into her bag, pulling out a guidebook. She quickly leafed through it. "It's on Pearl Street. That's downtown. But it looks like we can take a subway there. . . ."

"Yay! Let's do it!" Erin cheered.

"Why not?" Ms. Keatley said, as though she were convincing herself. "We've got to make the most of every minute here, right?"

"Awesome," Erin said. She held up her pizza slice. "A toast! To Ms. Keatley, the best advisor ever!"

"To Ms. Keatley!" the girls said, and they bumped their pizza slices together.

The Fraunces Tavern Museum looked out of place in downtown Manhattan. The three-story brick building on the corner of Pearl Street was dwarfed by the silver skyscrapers that towered over it.

"Whoa. It's like we stepped back in time," Erin said, looking up. "Check out that chimney. I bet this is the only building in Manhattan that still has a chimney."

"The guidebook says that it was built in 1719," Ms. Keatley reported. "It's one of the oldest buildings in New York."

They stepped inside. Behind the desk, a woman with short gray hair smiled at them.

"Are you interested in a tour?" she asked. "There's one starting in fifteen minutes."

"We're mostly here to see the jewelry exhibit," Erin said quickly.

"Of course. It's lovely," the woman said. She handed Ms. Keatley five pamphlets. "Here's some information about the pieces in the collection. Admission is free for students. The exhibit is just down the hall, first door on the right."

"Thanks!" Erin said with a grin.

Ms. Keatley paid for her admission, and as they walked to the exhibit, the Jewels passed a large room with weathered wood floors. A portrait of George Washington hung over the fireplace, and sconces on the walls lit up the room. A line of small tables with chairs stretched across the floor, and near the window was one long, wooden table.

"This must be the tavern part," Erin guessed. "Awesome. George Washington's butt might have touched one of those chairs!"

"Eww," Jasmine complained. "Can we please get to the jewelry now?"

She quickened her pace and the others followed her to the exhibit. The room had the same wood floors, but it was filled with rectangular glass cases set on wooden stands. A few visitors milled around, looking at the displays, and a security guard in a black uniform kept watch from the corner.

Jasmine made a beeline for the nearest case. "Oh my gosh. Look at these pearls," she said, breathless.

Lili joined her and looked into the case. "Wow, they're so creamy," she remarked.

Jasmine's eyes shone with excitement. She had been interested in gemstones since she was a little girl picking up pretty rocks in the park. She had collected rocks and gemstones ever since. They fascinated her. The science nerd in her loved to learn about their properties and what made a ruby red and an emerald green. But the rest of her just loved how beautiful they were.

Ms. Keatley handed each girl a pamphlet and then wandered over to the far side of the room. Willow and Erin approached Jasmine and Lili.

"We need to find the diamond earrings," she whispered, opening the pamphlet. She quickly scanned it, and then pointed to a photo on one of the pages. "Here they are. It says they belonged to a socialite who died in 1849. The designer of the earrings is unknown. But they think they could have been made as early as 1760."

"Then they could have belonged to Martha Washington," Erin pointed out. "These *must* be the ones!"

"They're over here," Willow said, leading the girls to a nearby case.

Behind the glass, the diamond earrings sparkled inside a box lined with black velvet.

"Gorgeous," Jasmine whispered. She jokingly flipped her curly hair behind her ear. "Don't you think they would look fabulous on me?"

"Definitely," Lili agreed.

"It's sad, in a way," Jasmine said. "Nobody will ever wear them again. They'll be stuck in this glass case forever."

"Speaking of the glass case, how do you think the Rivals plan to steal them?" Willow asked. "When they stole the ruby necklace, they didn't have to break into something like this." Willow ran her hand over the smooth pane of glass. "I don't see any way in. And look at that metal box inside. It seems like an alarm."

"Maybe they're going to break the glass and make a run for it," Erin suggested.

"It could be shatterproof, like the kind they use on windshields," Jasmine pointed out. "That would stop anyone from grabbing the earrings. But I guess we don't really know."

"We can find out," Erin said, eyeing the security guard.

Jasmine grabbed Erin's arm. "Erin, what are you thinking?"

"Relax," Erin told her. "We're just some inconspicuous sixth-grade girls."

The Jewels watched as Erin boldly strode up to the security guard.

"Excuse me, sir," she said politely.

The guard, a tall, burly man with dark hair, nodded. "Can I help you?"

"I'm doing a report for school," she said. "We're supposed to find out how the museum keeps the exhibit safe."

The man gave her a sympathetic smile. "Don't worry, young lady, this exhibit is one of the safest in New York City. The cases are made of shatterproof glass, and if anyone does breach the glass, an alarm goes off that's connected to the NYPD. If a thief got past me — and they wouldn't — they'd find the police waiting for them outside."

"That's good to know," Erin said. "Thanks!"

"Good luck with your report," the guard told her.

Erin turned back to her friends with a big smile on her face.

"You scare me sometimes," Lili said. "That was brilliant."

"And useful," Willow added with a thoughtful frown. "If these really *are* the Martha Washington diamonds, the Rivals will have to be geniuses to steal them!"

Chapter Six

The next morning the girls got in the line for the hotel's breakfast buffet, yawning and bleary-eyed.

"I don't think I can make it until Saturday," Lili said, leaning her head on Erin's shoulder.

Jasmine yawned in agreement. "I am soooooo tired."

Erin piled waffles onto her plate. "Yeah, but *Transformers: The Musical* was worth it. A show about singing, flying robots? We don't have anything like that in Hallytown."

The girls took their plates of food to one of the round tables in the hotel restaurant. Ms. Keatley was sitting across the room, talking to one of the other quiz bowl advisors she had met the night before.

"You know, I've been thinking," Willow began as they sat down.

"About flying robots?" Erin asked. "Because I was dreaming about those all night."

"No, about the earrings," Willow said. "I don't see how the Rivals can steal them. But we should keep an eye on them just in case."

"From a distance, I hope," Jasmine said.

Willow shook her head. "No. I'm thinking we should get Ms. Keatley to talk to Mr. Haverford and agree to do something on Friday."

Jasmine and Erin groaned, but Lili stuck up for Willow.

"I think it's a good idea," Lili said. "If we're with them, then they can't steal anything."

"Maybe they're planning to sneak out in the middle of the night," Jasmine pointed out.

"But they'd have to go through the lobby, and there's always someone at the desk," Willow argued. "Even if they didn't get stopped, they'd be caught on video camera. So if they do steal the diamond, we'd have proof."

Erin nodded. "It's a good plan," she said. "Let's go somewhere where we don't have to mingle too much, though."

"In the meantime, I can't stop thinking about that note you got on the train," Jasmine said. "Something is supposed to happen on 'Thursday at fifteen hundred hours.' That's today at three o'clock."

"And we don't know where to go or what to do!" Lili said with a frown.

Ms. Keatley walked up and sat down at the table with them.

"So what's on the agenda for today, girls?" she asked, taking a sip of coffee.

"Lots of naps," Jasmine suggested with a yawn.

Ms. Keatley laughed. "Yesterday was a big day. I was thinking we could get in some practice this morning, and then maybe work on your reports about the Fraunces Tavern before lunchtime. Then we've got the reception at five o'clock."

"Ooh, can we go to Central Park after lunch?" Lili asked, suddenly looking more awake.

"That's a lovely idea," Ms. Keatley said. "It will be nice to get out for a walk after being cooped up all morning."

"Yay! I'm sure I'll get some amazing photos," Lili said happily.

"Oh, and we were thinking we should take the Rivals up on their offer," Willow said. "Maybe we can do something on Friday together."

Ms. Keatley smiled. "That's very mature of you girls. What were you thinking?"

"Something fun," Erin suggested, digging into her waffles.

"How do you feel about ice-skating in Rockefeller Center?" Ms. Keatley asked. "That's one of those things everyone should do at least once."

Lili looked nervous. "Ice skate? I don't know how."

"I'll teach you," Erin promised. "Mary Ellen's been taking lessons since she was three, and Mom always drags me along. So I sort of learned by osmosis."

Lili sighed. "Okay. I guess I'll just wear lots of padding."

"I'll tell Josh," Ms. Keatley said. "And when you're finished eating, we'll go upstairs and start practicing for quiz bowl."

Three hours later the girls and Ms. Keatley sat in a café overlooking Central Park. A warm fire blazed in the cozy dining room. Roses decorated the curtains on the windows, and each ornate white metal chair had a pink cushion. They were eating bowls of tomato soup and sandwiches as they planned their walk through Central Park.

"There are so many beautiful sculptures!" Lili remarked, looking through Ms. Keatley's guidebook. "*Hans Christian Andersen and the Ugly Duckling. Balto the Sled Dog.* And *Alice of Wonderland,* of course. That one is amazing."

Ms. Keatley smiled. "'Twas brillig, and the slithy toves did gyre and gimble in the wabe," she recited with a dreamy look on her face.

The girls exchanged shocked glances. That was the verse from the message they'd received on the train!

"*What* did you just say?" Erin asked.

"'Twas brillig, and the —"

Willow interrupted her. "I think what Erin means to ask is *why* did you say that?"

"Because of the Alice statue," Ms. Keatley explained. "The verse is from Lewis Carroll's famous poem 'Jabberwocky,' and it's inscribed on the base of the statue."

The girls were bursting to talk to each other, but they couldn't — not in front of Ms. Keatley. Thinking quickly, Willow put her phone on her lap and began to text.

It's the message! We're supposed to meet at the Alice statue today at 3:00.

Jasmine texted back. *But ru sure we should go? We don't know who sent it.*

Maybe it was Ms. Keatley, Willow suggested. *Why else would she say that verse out of nowhere?*

OMG! That would be crazy, Lili typed. *How can we be sure?*

Ms. Keatley shook her head. "You girls and your cell phones. Honestly, I just don't understand it."

They quickly stopped texting and exchanged glances.

"Um, Ms. Keatley," Erin began with an innocent smile. "I was just curious, why did you start reciting that 'Jabberwocky' verse? Is there a, you know, *reason*?"

She emphasized the last word, hoping Ms. Keatley would reveal something. But the teacher had a blank expression on her face.

"Why, no," she said. "I memorized that poem when I was your age, and it was so tough, I guess I never miss an opportunity to recite it."

Willow and Erin locked eyes. Ms. Keatley seemed to be telling the truth.

So it's not *her,* Erin quickly texted everyone.

Then who? Jasmine asked.

Looks like we'll find out soon enough! Willow replied.

Chapter Seven

After lunch the girls and Ms. Keatley made their way down the tree-lined paths of Central Park. It was winter, so the branches were bare, but the twisting limbs looked beautiful against the crisp blue sky.

Ms. Keatley shivered in her black wool coat. "Well, I'm sorry, girls. It's a little colder than I thought it would be. How long would you like to spend out here?" she asked. "I wouldn't mind a cup of hot cocoa back in the hotel lounge right about now."

Willow checked the time on her phone. It was only two o'clock. She glanced at Lili with a look that said, *Can you answer this one?* Lili caught on and gave Willow a nod.

"I was hoping to see all of the sculptures on my list," Lili piped up. "Or at least some of them."

Willow grabbed Lili's guidebook and quickly calculated a route through the park that would take them to the Alice statue.

"We're not far from Strawberry Fields," Willow said. "Let's start there, head south, and then work our way back north."

Ms. Keatley perked up. "Strawberry Fields? I've always wanted to see the mosaic there. I'm a big John Lennon fan."

"Really?" Erin teased. "I thought you listened to colonial tea party music and stuff like that?"

The teacher smiled. "I appreciate John Lennon as much as I do John Adams."

They headed south on the path, warming up as they walked briskly toward their destination. The route took them past the lake in Central Park, where Canada geese spending the winter in the United States floated on the water's glassy surface.

Jasmine shook her head. "It's hard to believe there's a lake in the middle of a big city like this. It's as if we've been transported or something."

"Kind of like when we went to Fraunces Tavern yesterday," Erin said. "I bet there are little pockets like that all over the city, if you look for them."

They quickly reached Strawberry Fields, a section of the park dedicated to the memory of the musician John Lennon. A small crowd of people were gathered around the mosaic there, taking photos.

The girls made their way to the front of the crowd. The mosaic had been laid out on the ground, a circle of black and white stones surrounding a circle of white ones with the word IMAGINE in the center.

"It looks like a sunflower!" Jasmine realized. "I wonder what stone those tiles are made of?"

Lili began snapping pictures. "It's beautiful," she said. "I'd love to do a mosaic on the school lawn. Wouldn't that be awesome?"

"It would indeed, Lili," Ms. Keatley answered with a smile.

Willow glanced at the time. "Let's keep going, guys."

Luckily, spending an hour in the park turned out to be easy. There were so many things to look at. They passed the famous carousel with its beautifully painted horses. From there they headed north again to see the statue of Balto the sled dog, and then the majestic angel on top of Bethesda Fountain.

"We should be getting back to the hotel soon," Ms. Keatley said, rubbing her arms to stay warm.

"Just one more!" Lili pleaded. "The Alice statue is close by."

"Of course!" Ms. Keatley said. "We were just talking about that at lunch. Let's go."

They reached the statue just a few minutes before three o'clock. The bronze sculpture was an amazing sight — Alice perched on a giant toadstool, surrounded by the Mad Hatter, the March Hare, and the Cheshire Cat. And smaller toadstools invited children to climb and play with the storybook characters.

But even Lili didn't have her eyes on the sculpture just yet. The girls gazed around, looking for the mysterious person who had sent them the note. A girl who looked like a college student was sitting on a bench, sketching. Moms and nannies pushed by with strollers holding rosy-cheeked babies wrapped up in blankets. An elderly man walked slowly down the path using a cane, and two teenage boys on skateboards whizzed past him.

Enchanted, Ms. Keatley walked up to the Cheshire Cat, who sat on a tree stump behind the big mushroom, overlooking Alice. The girls huddled together and talked in whispers.

"What now?" Jasmine asked.

"I'm not sure," Willow said, looking around. "I don't see anyone who looks like they might have sent the message. Just a couple of moms pushing strollers."

"What about that old guy?" Lili suggested. "He looks kind of mysterious."

"But he's walking away," Willow pointed out.

"Maybe we're not supposed to meet a person," Erin suggested. "Maybe there's another message."

Willow nodded. "Let's look for another note on yellow paper."

The girls separated and walked around the statue, looking under the figures and mushrooms for any sign of a note. After a few moments Lili ran up to Willow and grabbed her by the arm.

"Follow me! I found something!" she said in an urgent whisper. Willow motioned for the other Jewels to follow them, careful not to draw Ms. Keatley's attention.

To the right of the statue, a yellow balloon waved in the air. At first it looked like it was tangled in the branches of a bush, but on closer inspection it appeared to have been deliberately tied there.

"It's yellow, like the paper," Lili said. "And look what somebody drew on it."

"A diamond shape!" Jasmine cried. "This must be from our mystery helper."

"I think I see something inside," Willow said. "We should carefully —"

POP! Erin had already stuck a pen into the balloon. The girls jumped at the sudden noise, and a yellow note floated to the ground.

Willow picked it up. "You scared me!" she told Erin.

"Sorry," her friend apologized. "What does it say?"

Willow read the message out loud. "Are you sure the diamond in the exhibit is the one the Rivals are after? History is the key."

Jasmine frowned. "So it's the wrong diamond?"

"I'm not sure," Willow said. "We need to study this more."

"Girls! Are you wandering off without me?" Ms. Keatley called out.

Willow quickly stuffed the note into her coat pocket. "Let's go. We can talk about this later."

The girls finally had a chance to discuss the note in their room that night, after the reception for the quiz bowl contestants. They had spent two hours eating tiny food off silver trays in a room filled with middle schoolers and high schoolers from the Northeast. By the time they got back to their suite, they were exhausted once again.

The Jewels sat in a circle on one of the beds.

"Wait. What if Ms. Keatley hears us?" Jasmine asked, worried.

"She can't hear regular talking through the walls," Erin pointed out. "Besides, she says she always reads before she goes to bed. Haven't you ever seen her when she's reading? She's like a zombie. It would take an explosion to get her away from a book."

Willow unfolded the note and placed it in the middle of the bed.

"So, I've been thinking," she said. "The note seems to be telling us that we might be looking at the wrong diamond. So that means there might be another diamond in New York that the Rivals are going to steal."

Erin jumped off the bed, rummaged through her overnight bag, and took out a small book with a leather cover.

"Here's that diary I told you about," she explained. "I've been thinking — the diamond in the tavern exhibit belonged to that family. Maybe I can find their name in the diary. That would link them, and then we could be sure it's the right diamond."

Willow nodded. "In the meantime, we can look for other diamonds in the city that might be from Martha Washington's time. Jasmine, you're our jewelry expert. Where else in New York would there be diamonds?"

"Everywhere," Jasmine said. "Museums. Shops. Exhibits. There's even a diamond district on Forty-seventh Street! It'll be like looking for a needle in a haystack."

"Or a diamond in Manhattan," Erin joked, carefully flipping through the pages of the diary. "I was just — wait, here's something."

Erin read from the diary page. " 'It is no longer safe to keep the four clues together. I have entrusted the most valuable of the four to John Townsend. As a Quaker, I know he can be trusted. He has promised to hide it most cleverly for me.' "

"What does that have to do with the diamond?" Lili asked.

Erin pointed to the page. "Well, she says there are four clues, just like there are four jewels. And she says they're valuable. So maybe the clues and the jewels are the same?"

Jasmine looked thoughtful. "Well, if that's true then she's probably talking about the diamond. It's possibly the most valuable of the four jewels."

Willow was already typing into her phone. "Okay, so here it says that John Townsend was a famous eighteenth-century furniture maker."

Lili began to bounce up and down on the bed. "The Met!" she cried.

"What about the Met?" Erin asked.

"The exhibit of colonial stuff, remember?" Lili asked. "There's tons of furniture there. And I remember reading the name Townsend on their website!"

Willow's brown eyes began to shine. "We may be on to something here," she said. "We've been looking for a diamond in plain sight. But the diamond could be hidden in the exhibit at the Met!"

Erin climbed off the bed and walked to the door.

"Where are you going?" Willow asked.

"To talk to Ms. Keatley," she said. "Sounds like it's time for a trip to the Met!"

Chapter Eight

"You girls certainly are keeping me busy," Ms. Keatley said the next morning as they walked up the stone steps to the Metropolitan Museum of Art.

"Well, we promised Principal Frederickson we'd have some educational experiences here. She'll love it if we visit another museum, won't she?" Willow suggested.

"Of course, of course," the teacher said. "But remember, we need to stay focused on tomorrow's competition. I want to make sure we get some practice time in today. We've got a lot scheduled."

"We won't be here long," Jasmine assured her.

Erin rubbed her gloved hands together. "And at least it's warm inside! I bet they sell hot chocolate here."

When they entered the museum, the blast of warm air was a welcome feeling. Inside, the huge main entrance hall was an impressive sight. Huge marble archways supported the dome-shaped ceiling, and sunlight streamed through the round window at the very top. The sound of visitors echoed through the massive space.

"We're looking for the exhibit of colonial furniture in the New American Wing," Lili told the woman behind the counter when they paid their admission.

The woman handed them a map. "Go through the Medieval Art hall to get to the New American Wing, and then take the escalator to the second floor. It's right here," she said, circling a portion of the map.

Lili smiled. "Thanks!"

"Colonial furniture," Ms. Keatley mused. "My, you girls really seem to be interested in the colonial period."

The girls froze and exchanged nervous glances. Maybe Ms. Keatley wasn't their mysterious messenger — but was she getting suspicious? They had never once questioned if their teacher knew that they were secretly trying to stop a group of sixth-grade jewel thieves in their spare time.

"It's because we go to Martha Washington," Erin offered. "It's like, in our blood or something."

The teacher smiled. "I know what you mean. Ever since I started teaching at the school, I've found that my interest in colonial American history has been piqued. It was such an exciting time for our country."

The girls breathed a collective sigh of relief. It seemed like their secret was safe from Ms. Keatley — at least for now.

They followed the map and quickly found the section of the New American Wing that featured the colonial furniture. Ms. Keatley quickly became absorbed in reading one of the information plaques, as she usually did when she got to a museum.

"We should have asked that lady down there where the Townsend furniture is," Jasmine said, as the girls slowly made their way through the exhibit of gleaming wood tables, desks, dressers, cabinets, and chairs.

"I didn't want to mention it — just in case we're on to something, you know?" Lili said. "Besides, it shouldn't be too hard to find."

The girls fanned out, scanning the plaques for John Townsend's name. It didn't take long before Jasmine motioned for the girls to join her.

"I think this might be it," she whispered. "I bet you could hide a lot of stuff in there."

She pointed to a desk behind the red velvet rope just in front of her. Made of golden brown wood, the bottom portion of the desk was a cabinet with nine drawers, three across and three down. The top part folded out on brass hinges, revealing more tiny drawers and cubby-holes. Three beautifully carved seashells decorated three wood panels in the front of the top portion.

"Wow, look at all those drawers," Lili said admiringly. "I could fit so many art supplies in there!"

Erin lowered her voice. "So, do you think the diamond could be in there somewhere?"

Willow nodded. "In her diary, Martha Washington said that Townsend was going to hide it for her. It makes sense that he would hide it in one of his pieces."

"So what now?" Jasmine asked. "We can't stand guard over it all the time. If the diamond is here, the Rivals could steal it, just like they stole the ruby."

"Good point," Willow said with a frown. "But even if we can't guard the diamond, we can still keep an eye on the Rivals. Like, Ms. Keatley made plans for us later."

Lili started snapping photos of the desk with her phone. "I'm going to take a lot of pictures. Maybe there's a clue somewhere that will tell us where the diamond is hidden."

"Good idea," Erin agreed.

Jasmine nervously gazed around the room, worried that they might be drawing attention to themselves. The security guard was an older man with a beard. He walked slowly up and down the exhibit, but didn't look interested in what the girls were doing at all.

But one visitor did seem attentive. Jasmine noticed that a short elderly woman kept walking back and forth, passing the girls each time. She wore a long, gray wool coat that matched her curly hair. She walked slowly, with a slight stoop.

Jasmine nudged Willow. "That old lady seems awfully interested in what we're doing," she whispered.

Willow casually glanced at the woman. Then her eyes narrowed.

"There's something really familiar about her," she said. "But I need to get a closer look. Do you have a pen on you?"

Jasmine rummaged through her bag and took out a pink marker. "How about this?"

"Perfect," Willow said.

Willow slowly walked up behind the woman. Just as the lady turned around, Willow dropped the marker a few feet in front of her. Then she bent down to retrieve it. When Willow picked it up, she was face to face with the woman, just like she had planned.

The old lady was wearing glasses, but Willow could recognize those brown eyes — and suspiciously *un*wrinkled face — anywhere.

"Oh, hi, Aaron," she said loudly. "Funny meeting you here!"

Aaron Santiago straightened up and took off his gray curly wig.

"Looks like you caught me," he said with a sheepish grin.

By now, Lili, Erin, and Jasmine had come running over.

"Caught you spying on us?" Erin asked.

Aaron laughed. "Are you guys still on that kick? No, I was just practicing my acting. When I'm not doing quiz bowl, I'm in the drama club, you know."

"Come on, Aaron," Willow accused. "It's so obvious you were spying on us."

"What for?" Aaron asked. "Are you doing something worth spying on?"

Willow bit her lip. Letting the Rivals know that they knew about the diamond would not be smart. She saw Erin open her mouth and nudged her before she could say anything.

Aaron grinned. He seemed to enjoy seeing Willow uncomfortable.

"I'm just trying out a new character," he said. "I'm pretty good at fooling people, you know."

"Yes, I know," Willow replied, looking him in the eyes. Just weeks ago, Aaron had disguised himself as a security guard at the Smithsonian Institution. He had fooled Willow then — and walked away with the Martha Washington ruby. But this time, she'd caught him.

Aaron's eyes twinkled. "I've fooled a lot of people in DC," he said, as though he were reading her mind. "So I thought, why not give it a try in the Big Apple? If I could pass for an old lady here, it would be genius."

Erin stepped up to face him. "I don't believe you for a second," she said. "You're here to steal that diamond."

The girls couldn't believe what Erin just blurted out. Willow sighed. Jasmine shook her head. Now the Rivals knew that the Jewels knew about the diamond. Talk about genius.

"Diamond? What diamond?" Aaron asked innocently, then smiled crookedly. "And even if I was, where's your proof?"

He put the wig back on and winked at them, then slowly shuffled away.

Jasmine threw her hands up in the air. "That's our problem. We never have any proof!"

Chapter Nine

"Erin, didn't you feel me nudge you?" Willow hissed when Aaron was out of earshot.

"Well, yeah, but I thought you were just bumping into me," Erin said. "Why?"

"Now the Rivals know that *we* know about the diamond," Willow explained. "It's going to be harder to stop them now! They're going to be watching our every move."

Erin blushed. "Oh, yeah. I guess I didn't think of that. Sorry."

"Well, look on the bright side," Lili said. "If he was trying to steal the diamond, we stopped him. That's what we're here to do, right?"

"But we're not even sure there's a diamond in that desk," Jasmine pointed out. "We're just guessing."

"Right, but the fact that we found Aaron here means we're on to something," Willow said firmly. "From now on, we need to stick to those Rivals like glue."

Erin raised her hand. "Dibs on anyone but Isabel!"

Lili laughed. "I agree. Erin and Isabel do not play well together!"

Erin sniffed. "As if she could play nice with *anyone*."

"We have our chance this afternoon," Willow reminded them. "We're all going ice-skating together!"

"As if I could forget," Erin rolled her eyes. "But we've got to do whatever we can to stop the Rivals — even if it means hanging out with them!"

After eating lunch at the museum's café and a quick stop at the hotel, they set off for Rockefeller Plaza.

"Josh said it would be easier if they just met us there," Ms. Keatley explained as they walked down Fifth Avenue. "He said that the kids had other plans earlier today."

The girls exchanged glances. They knew what Aaron had been up to. But what had the other Rivals been doing? Jasmine felt a pang of worry. What if they were wrong about everything?

But the sight of many different flags flapping in the breeze distracted her. They were at Rockefeller Center!

The flags, in a rainbow of colors, overlooked the sunken plaza and the ice skating rink below. A crowd of people were standing around and watching the skaters.

"Wow!" Willow said, impressed. "It looks just like it does on TV!"

Couples holding hands went gliding by on the ice below. They shared the ice with parents skating with their children, solo skaters, and groups of giggling teenagers. Some were experienced, while others held on to the rail along the sides of the rink. And above it all stood a giant golden statue of a man set in the middle of a cascading fountain.

"Prometheus!" Erin exclaimed. "He stole fire from Zeus to give it to mortals. At least, according to Greek mythology he did."

"Fire and ice, huh?" Lili wondered as she gazed out at the skaters. "Sounds like us and the Rivals!"

"And they're the icy ones," Jasmine chimed in. "Ice cold!"

"Yeah," Erin agreed. "And we're on fire with awesomeness!"

"Hey," Ms. Keatley said. "I thought you girls were trying to make peace by coming here."

Erin started to groan, but Willow jabbed her in the ribs. She quickly turned her groan into a cough.

Jasmine nodded. "You're right, Ms. Keatley. I was just joking around."

"Well then, let's go ice-skating!" Ms. Keatley said enthusiastically.

They walked through the outdoor gardens to reach the rink. At this time of year, the gardens were filled with fresh, sweet-smelling evergreen bushes and trees. When they reached the end, they climbed down the stairs to the skate house.

As Ms. Keatley paid for the skating session, Lili began to look anxious.

"What if I fall?" she asked nervously.

"You'll get back up again," Erin said confidently. "You'll be fine."

They rented ice skates and went to the locker room to change out of their shoes.

"This is even harder than it looks!" Lili said as she wobbled toward her friends. "And I'm not even on the ice yet!"

Finally, they stepped out onto the rink. Ms. Keatley began to glide slowly across the ice. "I haven't been skating in years," she said, a smile spreading across her face.

Willow and Jasmine followed behind her. "This is fun!" Jasmine said. She felt like she could skate away all her worries about the diamond.

Erin hung back with Lili, who was holding on to the rail as if her life depended on it.

"You can do it, Lili!" Erin cheered her on. "Move just a tiny bit away from the rail."

Lili let go and shuffled a few inches.

"I'm doing it!" she smiled.

Suddenly, a fast skater zoomed by and clipped her on the shoulder, sending Lili crashing onto the ice.

"Hey!" Erin yelled. "Watch where you're going!"

The skater swung around. It was Isabel!

"So sorry!" she said. "I knew we were supposed to go ice-skating with the Jewels, but I did not know the Jewels couldn't skate!" She glided off, and then made a graceful twirl before disappearing into the crowd.

Erin felt her face growing hot. "We can too skate!" she yelled after Isabel as she helped her friend up. "I'll show her."

Willow, Jasmine, and Ms. Keatley heard the commotion and came skating back.

"Lili, are you okay?" their teacher looked worried.

"I'm fine." Lili grinned. "Erin was right. If you fall, you just get back up again. My fear of falling on skates has been cured, thanks to Isabel."

Willow glanced up. The other Rivals were taking to the ice, along with their advisor. A big smile broke out on his face when he saw Ms. Keatley. Mr. Haverford came skating over, with a reluctant-looking Ryan, Aaron, and Veronica trailing slowly behind. Ryan seemed to have "bored" written over his face, Veronica's arms hung limply at her sides, and Aaron looked unsteady on his feet as he shuffled along.

"I'm so glad you could make it," Mr. Haverford said to Ms. Keatley.

Ms. Keatley smiled. "How can you visit New York in the winter without a spin around the world's most famous ice rink? It's an experience I'm glad to share with the girls."

"The girls? Oh, yes, of course," Mr. Haverford chuckled. He had clearly forgotten anyone else was there. "I was thinking, maybe the kids would enjoy going to the observation deck at Rockefeller Center later? I heard it can be very romant — I mean, fun."

Ryan looked at Willow and rolled his eyes. Then he grinned. Willow had to smile back. The only one who had no idea that Mr. Haverford was crushing on Ms. Keatley was Ms. Keatley herself!

"Um, maybe, if we have time," Ms. Keatley said absently as she skated toward Lili. "Come on, Lili, we'll have you skating like an Olympian before we leave." The two glided off together slowly, Lili continuing to wobble, and Mr. Haverford following behind.

Just then Erin let out an angry shriek and pointed to the middle of the rink. Both the Rivals and the Jewels turned to look at what had upset her.

Isabel was front and center, doing a perfect spin. A crowd of skaters had gathered around her to watch. She had on a pink skirt over black leggings. The skirt twirled beautifully as she turned on the ice.

"Ugh!" Erin said. "Why does she have to be so annoying all the time?"

Aaron laughed. "That's Isabel. She's pretty much perfect. And if you forget, she'll remind you."

Veronica let out a big sigh. "Whatever. I don't know why we had to come. I could be studying for quiz bowl instead."

Jasmine exchanged glances with Willow. It was weird, hanging out with the Rivals like this.

Erin looked over at Lili, who had gone back to slipping her way along the handrail. Lili's eyes seemed to be glued to Isabel as the Rival twisted and turned in graceful arcs. Lili was clearly too intimidated to try pushing off the rail again. It was time to take action.

"What's so fun about skating all by yourself?" Erin asked their small group. "It's conga time, people!"

"Conga?" Veronica asked in disbelief.

"Conga, conga, conga!" Erin sang out loudly. She grabbed Willow around the waist. "Conga line, right here!"

Willow sighed and started skating. She knew there was no stopping Erin when Isabel was involved.

Lili hung back, her eyes wide with fear.

"Grab on, Lili!" Erin urged her. "This is an easy way to learn without falling."

Jasmine skated up behind her. "You hold on to Erin, and I'll hold on to you. There's no way you can fall, promise."

"Well . . . okay," Lili said reluctantly, and soon their small conga line was weaving around the rink.

"Conga line!" a skater in the crowd cried out, and placed her hands around Jasmine's waist.

"Yes!" Erin yelled. "Come on, people. You're not cool if you're not in the conga line!"

A few of the skaters heard Erin, laughed, and joined in. As they skated around the rink, they picked up more and more people.

The chain of skaters glided around the edge of the ice. Isabel was still in the center, doing jumps and spins. But her audience was shrinking as the conga line grew.

"Jewels! Jewels! Jewels!" Erin started chanting. The conga line had no idea what she meant, but were having such a good time that they happily chimed in.

It was too much for Isabel. She stamped one skate-clad foot, pouted, and skated off the ice.

The other Rivals saw it as their chance to leave, too. They quickly followed Isabel toward the exit. Ryan turned and flashed another smile at Willow before leaving. It surprised her. She didn't trust him, and she was *definitely* going to try her best to stop whatever plan he had for the diamond. But for the first time she didn't find his smile totally annoying.

"I guess we're leaving," Mr. Haverford said to Ms. Keatley.

"Hmmm, what?" Ms. Keatley looked up from the conga line. "Oh, okay. Thanks. Have a good night."

"Maybe I can get a rain check on the observation deck?" Mr. Haverford asked hopefully.

"The what?" Ms. Keatley asked over the chanting. "Oh. I guess so, if we get a chance before the trip is up."

"Great!" The Rivals advisor smiled. "See you later!"

Since Lili was just getting the hang of it, they stayed and skated for a little longer before calling it quits.

"Skating *is* fun!" Lili said cheerfully in the locker room as they changed back into their shoes. "I'm no pro, but at least I know I can stand without falling now."

"You did awesome, Lil!" Erin said. "But I'm beat. Starting a conga line is hard work."

As Jasmine bent to tie her sneakers, a flash of yellow on the floor caught her eye. She got down on her knees and peered under the bench. It was a piece of yellow notebook paper, exactly like the one the other messages had been on! She grabbed it and sat back on the bench to read it.

"We've got another secret message!" she said excitedly. The Jewels gathered around. "But this one I don't get. It looks like a map of Central Park."

Willow snatched the note from her. "Huh," she said. "It is. Someone drew it on here." She pointed. "See — there is the Great Lawn. And these are the lakes and ponds."

Erin looked over Willow's shoulder. "How do we know a tourist didn't drop it? It could be just a coincidence that it's on the same yellow paper."

"Look at the lettering!" Lili pointed out. "It's the same handwriting that was on the first note, I'm sure."

Jasmine took the paper back from Willow and examined it closely. "And it says 'Saturday, nineteen hundred.' That's military time again, just like the second clue."

"Nineteen hundred means seven p.m.," Willow explained.

"There's more," Jasmine said as her eyes searched the drawing. "The letters V, A, I, and R are scattered on the map."

Willow looked thoughtful. "What does it mean? Is it another meeting time and place, like the *Alice in Wonderland* statue?"

"If it is, where are we supposed to meet?" Lili wondered.

"I'm not sure," Willow answered. "But I do know one thing. Tomorrow is Saturday. We don't have a lot of time to find out!"

Chapter Ten

While the Jewels were figuring out their latest clue in New York City, Eli Higashida, Lili's brother, was at an Atkinson Prep Computer Club meeting solving a puzzle of his own.

"I think we should go with Linux clusters over Windows," Eli said to his friend, Zane. "It's way more efficient."

"Yeah, you're probably right," Zane answered. "I still can't believe we're building a supercomputer. It's so totally cool. And it's awesome that Mr. Atkinson is donating old computers from the school that we can use!"

Eli nodded slowly. Even though it was generous of their headmaster to give the club the computers, Eli had information that Zane did not. At first, Eli had thought his little sister, Lili, was crazy when she told him that the Rivals had stolen the ruby from Martha Washington. When it all turned out to be true, Eli tried to help the girls get the ruby back. But the Rivals had foiled their plans. Eli knew the group of Atkinson sixth graders must have had help to pull off the jewel heist, and he suspected Arthur Atkinson had given it to them.

And is he helping them to steal even more jewels now? Eli wondered. Before she left for New York, Lili had told him the Jewels suspected the Rivals were going to strike again in New York City and steal a diamond. Eli sighed and ran his hand over his spiky black hair. All he wanted to worry about was joining a cluster of computers together to create one powerful supermachine — not his little sister getting mixed up with a gang of juvenile jewel thieves!

"Dude, I gotta go," Zane said, interrupting Eli's thoughts. "We're the last ones here, and my mom is going to pick me up any minute now."

"Sure, Zane," Eli said. "We're making progress. I'll see you tomorrow."

As Zane left, Eli rolled the cart that held the computer cages into the corner of the computer lab. He picked up his backpack and walked down the empty hallway toward his locker.

As he rounded a corner near Arthur Atkinson's office, he overheard voices.

"Mr. Atkinson, I don't understand," a man said. "You're being very generous, but this key is no good to you."

Eli stood still so he could listen. The man's voice was unfamiliar.

"I'm paying plenty for it, so you don't have to worry about what it's for," the headmaster said in his loud, confident tone.

"But Mr. Atkinson, this key is for a very specific desk, one that was built in the seventeen hundreds," the stranger said.

"So what is the problem, David? You are an antique furniture dealer. I want an antique key you have," Atkinson said. "I'm willing to pay top dollar for it, too. It seems simple to me."

"The desk I sold you last year was built in the eighteen hundreds," David explained. "This key won't work for it. It is for a specific desk that was built in the eighteenth *century*."

"Are you going to sell me the key or not?" Atkinson questioned, his voice rising with impatience.

"Of course, of course," the antiques dealer replied quickly, unwilling to lose the sale. "I simply wanted to make it clear that it would not work with your present desk."

"Understood. Thank you, David," Atkinson said firmly. "And as always, this transaction must be held in the strictest of confidence. Now, if we are finished here . . . ?"

"Yes, of course. Good night," David replied with relief. Eli heard a chair scraping against the floor, then footsteps.

He turned around quickly and pretended to be opening up a locker as the antiques dealer walked by. Then he casually walked past Arthur

Atkinson's office, glancing into the room. He saw the headmaster sitting at his desk, staring at the key he was holding in the palm of his hand. He didn't even look up as Eli passed.

That was weird, Eli thought as he picked up his pace and hurried to his own locker. *Why is Arthur Atkinson getting so worked up about a key? He was pretty mean to that dealer guy; the key must be important somehow. If Lili is right and the Rivals are planning another jewel heist in New York, the key could have something to do with it.*

He grabbed his phone out of his backpack and started texting his sister.

Vanishing jewels. Mysterious keys. It was much harder to figure out than building a Linux box from stock parts. Eli shook his head as he texted. He hoped the Jewels could get to the bottom of it!

Chapter Eleven

"Honestly, girls, I am beat." Ms. Keatley sounded tired as they walked into their suite after ice-skating. "I'm going to lie down for a few minutes before we eat, okay?"

Jasmine yawned. "That sounds like a good idea. I think I will, too."

"The quiz bowl dinner is at seven p.m.," Ms. Keatley reminded them. "Luckily, it's right here in the hotel, in the tenth floor ballroom. So we don't have far to go. We'll head down a few minutes before seven." She walked through her bedroom door and shut it behind her.

Jasmine opened the door to the girls' room and flopped onto the bed. Erin jumped next to her and picked up a pillow. "Pillow fight!" she teased.

Willow groaned as she sat on the bed next to them. "Seriously, like, no way! We're tired and we've got lots to talk about."

Lili kicked off her shoes and lay down next to Willow. "Erin, what are you, the Energizer Bunny?"

Erin grinned. "I'm just super-excited that I truly and totally bugged Isabel for the first time. Did you see her stomp off the ice? Ha!"

"Anyway," Willow said as Erin cackled with glee, "we've got a new message from our mystery helper to decipher. Any ideas?"

A beeping noise answered her. Lili grabbed her phone and read a text message. Her eyes widened.

"News from Eli!" she said. "It might be a clue, or it might not."

"Huh?" Jasmine asked. "What do you mean?"

Lili explained what Eli overheard. "So basically, Atkinson was acting really weird about a key for a seventeen hundreds desk."

"But the antique dealer said Atkinson owned a desk that was made in the eighteen hundreds," Willow pondered aloud. "What would he need another key for?"

"That's the question!" Erin explained. "Do you think it's possible the answer is the desk we saw in the Met?"

Jasmine bit her lip as she thought. "The John Townsend desk? Maybe, but it does feel like a stretch."

"Then the diamond could be in the desk after all!" Lili cried.

Willow tapped her fingers on the bed, pondering. "The desk wasn't behind glass, or protected by alarms."

"Nope! It just had a fancy red velvet rope in front of it," Erin said.

"Pretty easy. Wait until the security guard walks the other way and slip behind the rope. We've done harder stuff than that before!"

"Did anyone notice if the desk had any locks on it?" Jasmine asked.

Lili held up her phone. "No, but I took lots of pictures." She began to run her finger along the touch screen while squinting at the images.

"It's hard to tell on the phone," she said "Let me e-mail them to my computer, and I'll open them up with the photo program."

She pulled her laptop out of a dresser drawer, plugged it into the wall behind the bed, and sat back down. The girls gathered around her.

Lili opened up the photos. She flipped through until the she found the best shot, and then zoomed in on the brown desk.

"There!" she said as she pointed at the screen. "The top part!"

The top of the desk folded down to reveal tiny drawers and cubbyholes. Lili had zoomed in on the left side, where one of the small drawers had a keyhole on the front.

"There it is!" Erin cried as she pointed.

They gazed at the screen silently for a few moments.

Jasmine broke the silence. "So the diamond the Rivals are after could be in that locked desk drawer?"

"It could be. Or the diamonds they are after really are the earrings at the Fraunces Tavern Museum," Erin moaned. "This is so hard!"

"If Arthur Atkinson has the key, when — or how — is he going to get it to the Rivals?" Willow asked.

Lili chimed in. "But doesn't it seem like way too much of a coincidence? Martha's diary, the Townsend desk, bumping into Aaron at that exhibit, Atkinson getting a mysterious key, and now a locked drawer?"

"It's a lot to think about," Erin said. "And you know I can't think on an empty stomach! Isn't it almost time to eat?"

Willow sighed, stood up, and stretched. "Erin's right. We should get ready for dinner. But we've gotta keep a close eye on the Rivals. Be on the lookout for Arthur Atkinson or any mysterious packages!"

"Yes, sir!" Erin stood up straight and saluted Willow.

They all burst out laughing.

"Someone's got to keep our spirits up," Erin said. "It might as well be me!"

They got ready and met a refreshed Ms. Keatley before taking the elevator down to the tenth floor. The elevator stopped once to let on another group of quiz bowl students and their teacher, chatting excitedly. The smell of food greeted them as the elevator doors opened on the tenth floor.

They walked into the ballroom, which doubled as a conference room. A floral carpet in shades of blue, red, and gold covered the floor, and several glass chandeliers adorned the ceiling. A large buffet service was set up against one wall, and tables and chairs filled the rest of the room. Students and their teachers were checking in at a table just inside the door.

Ms. Keatley signed them in and each of the Jewels received name tags.

"Let's eat!" Ms. Keatley said. "And don't forget about mingling with some of your quiz bowl competition. It's nice to meet other —" But Erin was already making her way to the buffet. Ms. Keatley laughed and shook her head as they got in line behind her.

"Salad! Ziti! Chicken parm!" Erin announced each food as she piled it on her plate. "Meatballs!" she chirped as she reached her hand out for the serving spoon, but at the same exact moment someone else was reaching for it, too. She quickly drew her hand back and looked up. A boy with brown hair, wearing glasses and a buttoned-up shirt, held the spoon.

"Hey!" Erin said. "Don't mess with my meatballs" — she read his name tag — "George!"

"Sorry!" George took his hand off the spoon. "I love meatballs. But

then again, I love ziti. And salad. And chicken parmesan. Here."
George moved out of the way. "There's plenty."

Erin smiled and served herself some meatballs. "I know what
you mean. Walking around New York really builds up an appetite,
doesn't it?"

"Definitely," George agreed. "Besides, I always think better on a
full stomach. I need to keep up my energy for quiz bowl."

"Hey, that's what I always say!" Erin said, impressed. "So, where
are you from?" The two chatted as they made their way down the rest
of the buffet line.

Lili whispered into Jasmine's ear. "I think Erin has found her
soul mate."

They all filled up their plates and found an empty table. George
and one of his quiz bowl partners, Lauren, joined them.

"George and Lauren are from Pennsylvania," Erin explained. The
Jewels were enjoying eating and talking with their new friends until
the Rivals entered the room. Willow nudged Jasmine in the side and
pointed as a reminder to keep an eye on them.

The rest of the evening passed quickly. The girls met some of the
other team members, a few of the quiz bowl coordinators made
speeches — and the Jewels were watching the Rivals the entire time.
Nothing exciting happened, except Ryan spilling his drink.

Finally, dessert was served. Erin and George were the first in line for the cake and cookies. The other girls filed in right behind the Rivals, who didn't seem to see them.

Aaron and Ryan were joking around with each other, while Isabel was talking to Mr. Haverford.

"I need to go back to the Fraunces Tavern Museum tomorrow, Mr. Haverford," she said loudly. "It's an emergency!"

Mr. Haverford frowned. "Isabel, it's all the way downtown, and the quiz bowl tournaments start tomorrow."

"I left my cell phone there!" Isabel whined. "We have a break during the afternoon tomorrow. Can't I go then? It's a really expensive phone. My father will be very angry if I don't get it back."

Mr. Haverford sighed. "We'll see."

Willow, Jasmine, and Lili exchanged looks and rushed back to the table where Erin was eating cake with George.

"We need you!" Lili said. "Privately! Just for a sec. Sorry, George."

"No problem," he said, getting up from the table. "I was just going up for seconds."

"Grab me some, too, please!" Erin called after him, then turned to her friends. "So what's up?"

Jasmine quickly filled her in on what they had overheard.

Willow snapped her fingers. "I just remembered something! When we were skating, before you started the conga line, Isabel pulled her phone out of her jacket pocket and took a picture of herself in front of the *Prometheus* statue."

Willow took out her own phone and typed something in. "Aha!" She had gone to Isabel's Chatter profile. "Look at her profile pic!"

It was Isabel at the skating rink!

"She went skating *after* she visited the museum!" Lili said. "So she's lying about leaving her phone there."

"Then is she planning to steal the diamond from the jewelry exhibit tomorrow?" Erin asked.

"Maybe Aaron followed us to the Met just to throw us off the trail," Willow suggested. "And they've actually been planning to steal the diamond earrings from the Fraunces Tavern Museum this entire time."

Jasmine frowned. "Isabel was talking really loudly. Maybe she *wanted* us to hear her. The Rivals have set traps for us before."

"So you're saying Isabel's acting like she's got some big, secret reason to go back to Fraunces Tavern just to fool us?" Lili asked.

"Then that would mean the diamond is really hidden in the desk at the Met," Willow said thoughtfully.

Erin groaned and put her head down on the table. "This is so confusing!"

"There's only one way to know for sure," Willow said. "We've got to follow Isabel. If it's a trick, we'll just be embarrassed. But if we're wrong, then we'll lose the diamond, just like we lost the ruby!"

Chapter Twelve

"No way, Lili," Willow protested. "We are *not* wearing those!"

"For once, I might have to agree," Erin said.

"I don't know," Jasmine thought aloud. "I kind of like them."

It was seven o'clock the next morning, and the girls were up bright and early to get ready for the competition. Lili was practically jumping up and down with excitement as she showed her friends her latest creation: four matching tiaras to wear during their matches.

"But I worked so hard on them!" Lili pleaded. "I found plain silver tiaras at the accessories store at the mall, then spray-painted them to look just like the Statue of Liberty's crown. And I added some fake rubies, 'cause we're the Jewels. See?"

"They're pretty," Willow admitted. "But crowns? We're quiz bowl contestants, not princesses."

"We need to look like a team," Lili argued.

"A team of *princesses*," Erin countered sarcastically.

Jasmine stood up for Lili. "We do call ourselves the Jewels. It kind of goes."

Willow turned to Ms. Keatley. "We've got a tie. What do you think?"

Ms. Keatley held up her hands. "I'm staying out of this. Now let's get down to breakfast. We don't want to be late."

"Well, I'm wearing my crown," Lili said, planting it on top of her black hair.

"Me, too!" Jasmine said, sticking the tiara into her curly locks.

"I'm still not wearing mine," Willow said stubbornly.

"Me, neither," added Erin.

Lili tucked the other two into her bag. "Whatever. I'm bringing them, just in case."

The girls and Ms. Keatley left the room and got into the elevator. The door opened two floors down and George and Lauren, whom they had met the night before, got on with their teammates.

George grinned at the girls. "Nice tiaras," he told Lili and Jasmine.

"Yeah, they're really cool," agreed Lauren.

Lili beamed. "Thanks! I made them myself. For our team. 'Cause we're the Jewels."

Jasmine shot Willow and Erin a look. With a sigh, the girls each held out a hand. Lili smiled, opened her bag, and triumphantly handed them each a tiara.

Erin put hers on and glared at George. "Thanks a lot," she complained.

"What did I say?" he asked innocently.

The elevator opened up and the smell of bacon and eggs greeted them, reminding the girls how hungry they were. As they walked through the lobby toward the breakfast buffet in the dining hall, they saw Ryan Atkinson at the front desk.

"Here's your package, Mr. Atkinson," the woman said, handing him an envelope.

Curious, Willow walked closer to the desk. There was an overnight label on the envelope, as well as the logo of Atkinson Preparatory School.

Ryan caught Willow looking.

"Hey there," he said, startling her.

"Oh, hi," Willow replied. "Um, just wanted to say, good luck today."

Ryan grinned. "We don't need it," he replied, and Willow was instantly mad at herself for ever thinking that Ryan could be nice.

She turned and quickly caught up to her friends.

"What was that about?" Jasmine asked.

"I'll tell you guys later," Willow said, flustered. "I was just checking something out, that's all."

After breakfast they all took a short but brisk walk to Kane College, which was loaning out its auditorium for the day's competitions.

"So, the middle school qualifying matches are this morning," Ms. Keatley explained. "If we make the semifinals, we'll have a match around four o'clock. Then the final rounds take place tomorrow."

When they got to the large auditorium, it was quickly filling with quiz bowl teams from the region. Some teams wore matching T-shirts, while others, like the Rivals, wore their school uniforms to compete. One team even wore matching red scarves.

"See?" Lili said, pointing to them. "We're not the only ones."

They took their seats in the auditorium to watch the first round of competition. George and Lauren's team was facing a group from Delaware. The Jewels played along, whispering answers to the questions they knew. Their new friends won easily, and the Jewels cheered loudly for them.

The second match took place between the Rivals and a team from Queens, New York. Every time the moderator asked a question, one of the Rivals buzzed in before he even finished talking. The Queens team didn't have a chance.

"They're on fire," Willow whispered to Jasmine.

Erin shook her head. "It's a massacre. I feel sorry for that other team."

Then it was the Jewels' turn. They took their place on stage across from their competition. Each contestant stood behind a lectern with a microphone and a buzzer.

The girls looked at each other as the moderator got ready to begin.

"Oh, no! We forgot to do our pre-match cheer!" Jasmine said.

"We have time," Erin said quickly, thrusting out her hand. The other girls quickly gathered around her and placed a hand on the pile.

"Go, Jewels!" they cheered in a loud whisper.

A creaking sound echoed through the auditorium as the moderator adjusted his microphone. "And now, let's begin our match between the Martha Washington Jewels and the Maplewood Brain Busters," he said. "The questions in this round are worth five points each. First question: What natural phenomenon do seismologists study?"

Jasmine quickly hit her buzzer.

"Martha Washington," the moderator said with a nod to Jasmine.

"Earthquakes!" Jasmine answered, and the crowd in the auditorium clapped. Jasmine grinned at Willow, and they were both thinking the same thing. This was a good start to the match!

Both teams answered quickly. Willow aced a question about prime numbers, and Erin buzzed in on almost every history question.

"What is the name of the schoolmaster protagonist in the story 'The Legend of Sleepy Hollow'?" the moderator asked.

One of the Brain Busters buzzed in. "Washington Irving."

"Incorrect," said the moderator. "Martha Washington?"

Lili buzzed. "Ichabod Crane," she said, and the moderator nodded.

"Correct."

The questions kept coming, and the Jewels managed to stay one step ahead of their opponents. In the end, they beat the Brain Busters by a full twenty points. Ms. Keatley was waiting for them when they left the stage.

"Wonderful job, girls!" she congratulated them. "This means you're in the semifinals."

Willow held up her hand and high-fived her friends, one by one.

"We did it!" she cheered.

Ms. Keatley glanced at her watch. "We have a few hours until our semifinal match. There's a free lunch for the teams in the cafeteria here. Afterward we can watch the other teams compete, or take a walk, if you'd like."

Willow looked at her friends. They had been so caught up in the competition, that they had nearly forgotten Isabel's plan to go to Fraunces Tavern.

"What are the Rivals doing?" she asked innocently.

"I'm not sure," Ms. Keatley replied. "They left the auditorium right after your match."

Isabel's probably on her way to the museum, Willow thought, and she knew the other Jewels were thinking the same thing.

"Ms. Keatley, I lost my cell phone at Fraunces Tavern the other day," Erin spoke up. "I was wondering if we could go back and get it."

Ms. Keatley frowned. "I'd rather not have to take a subway ride. We need to be sure we're here for our semifinal match. And anyway, how can you be sure it's there? And why didn't you say you'd lost it earlier?"

Erin thought quickly. "I called them this morning. They said they have it," she lied. "It's not that far, and we have like, three hours."

Ms. Keatley sighed. "I suppose we must. Let's go now and eat when we get back."

She walked ahead of them down the auditorium aisle, shaking her head. Lili quickly sidled up to Erin.

"Lost cell phone? Why'd you use Isabel's excuse?" she asked.

Erin shrugged. "It worked for her."

Willow grinned. "So you're saying that Isabel had a good idea."

"I am not!" Erin protested. "And anyway, it worked. If Isabel is on her way to steal the diamond, then we'll be there to stop her!"

Chapter Thirteen

The subway ride downtown didn't take long, and soon they were walking down Pearl Street with Fraunces Tavern in sight.

"When we get in, Erin, you can go right to the front desk and get your cell phone," Ms. Keatley said. "And then we should head right back."

Lili turned and looked at her friends, frowning. The cell phone excuse had sounded like a good idea, but if they left right away they wouldn't be able to find out what Isabel was up to.

Willow was trying to think of a reason to ask Ms. Keatley if they could stay longer when an unexpected encounter saved them.

"Kelly! What are you doing here?"

Mr. Haverford walked toward them, waving.

"Josh!" Ms. Keatley looked surprised. "Erin left her cell phone here, and we came to get it."

Mr. Haverford shook his head. "What do you know? Isabel did the same thing. These kids and their cell phones, right? They're always losing things."

"Yeah, we're super-absentminded," Erin agreed, grateful that the advisors weren't suspicious.

"So Isabel's inside?" Willow asked.

Mr. Haverford nodded. "Yes, the others are studying with the team from south Jersey. The advisor and I are old friends. So I brought Isabel here."

"Why don't you two wait out here while we go get my cell phone?" Erin suggested.

"Oh, I don't mind coming in," Ms. Keatley said.

"Stay here with me. I need the fresh air," Mr. Haverford urged, flashing a grin.

Ms. Keatley shrugged. "Well, I suppose . . ."

Jasmine rolled her eyes. "How does she not know he's flirting?" she whispered to Willow.

"Who knows," Willow whispered back. "Now's our chance. Let's go!"

They entered the museum and nodded politely to the woman at the desk. They went straight to the jewelry exhibit, and just as they suspected, Isabel was hovering near the case with the diamond earrings. She was facing away from the door, and the girls hung back so they wouldn't be noticed.

"It doesn't look like she's searching for her cell phone," Jasmine hissed.

"No, it looks like she's going to steal the diamond!" Erin said.

"But how?" Willow asked. "The security guard's right there."

She nodded at the guard, the same tall, burly man that Erin had spoken to the last time they were there. As if on cue, the radio on his belt began to buzz and beep. He held it up to his mouth, said something, then got a puzzled look on his face. He quickly scanned the room as if to make sure everything was okay. Then he ducked through the door behind him into the next exhibit.

Isabel watched the guard leave. As soon as he was out of sight, she took off a chain that hung around her neck. Dangling from the end was a key!

Willow pulled the girls away from the door.

"Maybe it's a key that opens the jewelry case," she said excitedly.

"Arthur Atkinson just got an old key, remember?" Jasmine asked. "What if it's the same key?"

"You know, it could be," Willow said. "I've been meaning to tell you. Ryan received an overnight package from Mr. Atkinson just this morning."

Erin peered through the door.

"The security guard's not in the room, so it's perfect timing," she said. "We've got to stop her!"

"How?" Lili asked.

Willow looked thoughtful. "Erin, go find the security guard. The rest of you, follow me."

"Got it!" Erin said.

She raced through the door, and the rest of the Jewels followed Willow into the exhibit. This time, Isabel saw them. She turned around, dangling the key in her fingers.

"The Jewels! What could you possibly be doing here?" she asked, smiling.

"You know what," Jasmine replied angrily. "You're trying to steal those diamond earrings, but we won't let you!"

Erin came back in the room with the security guard behind her.

"That's her!" she said, pointing to Isabel. "She's got the key to that jewelry case and she's going to steal the diamond earrings!"

"That's a very serious accusation," the guard said. He sounded stern, but there was a twinkle in his eye that hinted he might have thought the whole situation was amusing. Nevertheless, he nodded to Isabel.

"May I see the key?" he asked.

"Oh, this key?" Isabel asked innocently. "This is the key to my diary."

She opened her bag and took out a leather-bound diary with a small lock. Then she used the small, silver key to open it.

"See?" she asked. "I must keep it locked, because I have many secrets in here."

She looked Willow right in the eyes when she said those words, and Willow knew right then that the Rivals were toying with them.

The security guard put a hand on Erin's shoulder. "Thank you for your concern, miss. I appreciate your vigilance. But it seems like everything's fine."

Erin's green eyes were blazing with fury. "Right. Fine," she said, her mouth tight.

Willow grabbed her arm. "Come on, let's go."

Angry and embarrassed, they marched down the hallway to the exit. Outside, Ms. Keatley was still talking to Mr. Haverford.

"Did you get your cell phone?" she asked Erin.

"Yeah. Got it. Whatever," Erin grumbled. "Thanks."

"What about Isabel?" Mr. Haverford asked.

The sun glinted off Isabel's blond hair as she bounded past them, grinning happily.

"I found it!" she said.

"Great!" Mr. Haverford exclaimed. "Now we can all take the subway back uptown together."

"How nice," Isabel said, flashing an evil grin at the Jewels.

The two teachers began walking toward the subway, and Isabel joined them with a skip in her step.

"I'd rather walk a hundred blocks than ride the subway with her," Erin moaned.

"They've tricked us again!" Jasmine said.

"So if Isabel didn't steal the earrings, then maybe the diamond is in the desk after all," Willow said thoughtfully.

Jasmine grumbled. "You know what that means. The other Rivals could be stealing it right now!"

Chapter Fourteen

The girls huddled together in a subway car, frantically trying to figure out what to do.

"Mr. Haverford said that the other Rivals were studying with another team," Willow pointed out. "So they couldn't be stealing the diamond."

"Unless Mr. Haverford is lying!" Jasmine accused. "Maybe he's in on it, too. The other Rivals are probably at the Met right now, stealing the diamond in the desk!"

She put her head in her hands. "Once again, we've messed up."

Erin nudged her. "Don't let Isabel see you like that. We've got to be cool. Act like it doesn't bother us."

"Erin's right," Willow said. "Maybe this was a plan to distract us. Or they might just be trying to discourage us from figuring out their real plan. If that's true, then we need to show them they didn't get to us."

"Right!" Lili agreed. "But maybe we should go to the Met as soon as we get back. You know, just in case."

Willow nodded. "Let's ask Ms. Keatley. But we should wait until we get off the subway. I don't want Isabel to hear us."

They exited the subway just a few blocks from the college. The girls waited until Mr. Haverford and Isabel waved good-bye and walked away, and then approached Ms. Keatley.

"Ms. Keatley, could we go back to the Met for the rest of the break?" Jasmine asked. "After all, we'll be busy with quiz bowl all day tomorrow, and then we have to leave."

Ms. Keatley shook her head. "Absolutely not. I want you girls to be focused and ready for the semifinals. Right now we're going to the school's cafeteria to eat, and then I want everyone to either relax or study."

The teacher's voice was firm, and the girls knew there was no use arguing. They reluctantly followed her to the cafeteria for lunch. But their mood improved after plates of salad from the salad bar.

"That was delicious," Ms. Keatley said, wiping her mouth with a paper napkin. "Now I think we all need to relax for a bit. Some of the advisors were talking about getting together in the auditorium for a little while to trade stories. But if you'd rather go back to the hotel . . ."

"That's fine," Willow said quickly. "We'll hang out in the auditorium. I can look up some quiz questions on my phone and we'll practice."

"Wonderful!" said the teacher, glancing at her watch. "Let's head there, then. The first semifinal match starts in about an hour. It should be interesting to watch."

Back in the auditorium, the girls found a quiet corner and sat cross-legged on the carpet, in a circle. Jasmine was still glum.

"It's like we're trapped here," she said. "The Rivals have beaten us again."

"Maybe," Willow admitted. "But maybe not. I think we should look at the clues. We need to figure out what's really happening."

"Okay," Jasmine said, taking a deep breath. "First, Lili got a message saying that the Rivals were going to steal the diamond, one of the four Martha Washington jewels. It said the diamond was in New York."

Willow nodded. "So then we researched," she said. "And you found out about the exhibit, Jasmine. It looked like the diamond earrings might be the ones. But we got a message saying that we could be wrong."

"And then I found the diary entry from Martha that said she gave the most valuable jewel to John Townsend, a furniture maker," Erin added. "And we found a desk made by him in the Met."

"And then Eli sent me a text that Arthur Atkinson got a key for an eighteenth-century desk," Lili continued. "And then Ryan got a package from Arthur this morning. And chances are it's the key."

Willow took a piece of yellow paper from her bag. "We forgot this message. The map."

She placed the paper on the floor in the middle of them.

"We're pretty sure it's a map of Central Park," Willow said.

Lili rummaged through her bag. "There's one in my guidebook. Let's compare them."

Lili quickly found the map in the book. "Okay, it's definitely the park. See that square on the map we found? That's the Met, over on Eighty-second Street."

The girls leaned in to get a better look.

"There's a letter R right by the square," Willow pointed out. "And then the I is next to the obelisk, and the V is by the Alice statue, and the A is over near Strawberry Fields."

"Maybe the letters form a word," Erin suggested. She wrinkled her nose as she thought. "Riva? Avir? Doesn't make sense."

"Maybe the letters stand for initials," Lili said.

"Then wouldn't there be a D by the museum?" Willow asked. "D for diamond?"

Jasmine's eyes lit up. "Unless it's a person. R — for Ryan!"

The friends exchanged excited looks. Jasmine was on to something!

"That's it!" Erin exclaimed in a loud whisper. "And the I is for Isabel, the V is for Veronica, and the A is for Aaron!"

"So why are they scattered all over the map like that?" Lili asked.

"I think I know," Willow said. "Remember at the Smithsonian, when Aaron took the ruby from me? Well, he ran through the museum and handed it to Isabel, and then she gave it to Ryan, and he ran out of the building."

Erin nodded. "I get it. They like to hand it off, to confuse whoever might be on to them. So do you think this is the same kind of plan?"

"It makes sense," Willow said. She put her finger on the R. "Ryan steals the diamond at the Met. He goes outside and meets Isabel at the obelisk."

"Oh, I know the obelisk," Lili interrupted. "It's from Egypt. It's really tall and skinny with a point on top. That's why they nicknamed it Cleopatra's Needle."

Willow nodded. "Right. It's a pretty obvious meeting spot. Then, check it out. Isabel runs down this path and hands it off to Veronica at the Alice statue. Then she goes across the park and gives it to Aaron, who takes it right to the hotel."

Jasmine looked worried. "That's got to be it. But what if they've done it already?"

Lili and Erin frowned. They hadn't thought of that. But Willow shook her head. "We forgot about this."

She pointed to the writing across the top of the map: *Saturday 1900.*

"We figured out that it's military time again, right? So that's seven p.m.," Willow said.

"Then they're going to do it tonight!" Erin yelled, and Willow motioned for her to be quiet. Erin lowered her voice to a whisper. "So what do we do? Steal the diamond before they can?"

Jasmine moaned. "That would be way too stressful. Besides, they have the key, and we don't."

Lili leaned in, her eyes wide with excitement. "We could hide in the museum and take a video of Ryan stealing it," she suggested. "Then we could show Principal Frederickson when we get home. She'd have to believe it if she saw a video."

"That's a pretty good idea," Willow said, and Lili smiled.

"It is," Erin agreed. "But we're forgetting one thing. These jewels are important somehow. Martha Washington said so. She even called them 'clues,' right? So if the Rivals get the diamond, even for a little while, they might be able to figure out the clues. And I don't want them to do that."

"Maybe, but there's no other way," Jasmine pointed out.

Erin grinned. "The Rivals fool us all the time," she said. "But I think I know a way we can finally fool them."

Jasmine tilted her head. "I like the sound of that."

"We'll need Eli's help," Erin said. "And Lili, I need to borrow some of your clothes. . . ."

The girls huddled together, whispering, until the competition started up once again. They tried to focus and relax while the first two teams went head to head, but each of them kept thinking about their plan. Would it work?

Then they heard applause, and the moderator's voice.

"Will the Martha Washington team and the Allentown All-Stars please join us onstage?"

"The Allentown All-Stars?" Erin asked. "Wait, that's George and Lauren's team!"

The girls' new friends from Pennsylvania waved as they headed up onstage. They were joined by their other two teammates.

Lili sighed and put on her tiara. "They're so nice. I'll feel bad if we beat them."

"There are no feelings in quiz bowl!" Willow reminded her. "Just victory. Let's do this!"

Each of the other Jewels put on her tiara and ran up to the stage to take her place. This time, they didn't start out as strong. Erin guessed that the capital of Washington was Seattle (instead of Olympia), and Jasmine said that the fibula bone in the leg was bigger than the tibia (instead of the other way around).

"Come on, guys," Willow hissed to her teammates. "We've got to stay focused!"

The Jewels rallied, and they managed to beat the All-Stars by five points. When the match was over, George and Lauren came across the stage to shake hands.

"You guys were tough to beat," Erin admitted.

"I know," George said with a laugh. "So you must be good."

"Just do us a favor, okay?" Lauren asked. "Beat those Rivals in the finals. Those guys are jerks."

Erin laughed. "Hey, they're not in the finals yet."

"I'm sure they will be," Willow said.

And of course she was right. The Rivals faced a team from Delaware and beat them easily. There was one more semifinal match after that, and then it was time for a dinner break and the regionals party.

"I'm so proud of you girls," Ms. Keatley said, giving them

high fives. "Your hard work is done for the day. Tomorrow, we face the finals."

"And the Rivals," Erin added, smiling at her friends. She knew they were all thinking the same thing.

But first, we have to face them tonight!

Chapter Fifteen

"It's a good thing they scheduled this party in the park tonight," Jasmine whispered to Willow.

Willow looked around the small area of the park that had been decorated with white twinkling lights and vendors handing out steaming mugs of cocoa. The "Night in the Park" quiz bowl party was scheduled from six thirty to eight — and the timing couldn't have been more perfect.

"Definitely," Willow agreed, looking at her watch. "Now let's get into position."

In the Metropolitan Museum of Art, Ryan Atkinson strolled around the colonial furniture exhibit, trying to look casual. He glanced at his watch. 6:58. The security guard should be leaving any minute now.

Ryan kept looking at the guard, a man of average height wearing glasses. Exactly at seven o'clock, he quietly strolled away from the exhibit.

Ryan grinned. His uncle Arthur had arranged things perfectly, as always. He had been hoping to get rid of the guard earlier, when Isabel was distracting the Jewels at the museum, but the crooked guard's shift had moved up. It ended up working out better than expected. The museum was open until nine on Saturdays, and nobody would miss the Rivals at the crowded quiz bowl party — especially not Mr. Haverford. Ryan knew he'd be busy talking to that Ms. Keatley the whole time. That wasn't part of the plan, but it was an extra lucky break for the Rivals.

Sometimes he didn't know how his uncle did it. It was a little scary that Arthur Atkinson seemed to have contacts everywhere. But that didn't matter — just as long as they got the diamond. Soon, the Rivals would be one step closer to returning all its old glory to Atkinson Prep.

Ryan quickly scanned the exhibit, which was mostly empty. A few people were strolling around, and Ryan didn't see any of the Jewels anywhere. Of course, he wasn't really expecting them — they were smart, but not smart enough to discover the exact place and time of the theft, Ryan was certain. He was sure that Isabel's little trick this afternoon had discouraged them, just like it was supposed to.

He couldn't help grinning, thinking about the Jewels. Uncle Arthur was convinced they knew the secret of the four Martha Washington jewels, and it looked like he was right. As soon as he sent them that message about the diamond they had started narrowing down its location. And after that message in the balloon, they had led the Rivals right to the desk. It was almost too easy! With any luck, getting the emerald would be just as simple.

Better focus! Ryan told himself. *That guard will be back in five minutes.* From his pocket, he quickly slipped out the key his uncle had given him. Then he stepped up to the desk, easily reaching over the velvet rope. The hidden keyhole was in the third drawer from the left.

He felt with his fingers until he touched the lock. Then he slipped in the key.

Success! A tiny hidden door slid open, and Ryan felt something inside. When he removed his hand he saw two sparkling diamond earrings in his palm.

With a grin, Ryan carefully placed them in a small velvet pouch he had brought with him and then stuffed it into his front jacket pocket. He slid the drawer closed and left the exhibit. He tried to walk slowly, but his heart was pounding and his palms were sweating. Even though he was sure no one had seen him, he wouldn't feel relaxed until he was out of the museum.

Ryan took the escalator to the first floor, looking left, right, up, and down for any sign of the Jewels or a museum guard on his tail. So far, so good. He made his way to the exit and held his breath until he was standing outside on the front steps in the chilly air. Then a smug smile spread across his face.

Perfect! Of course, he congratulated himself as he bounded down the stairs. Then he picked up his pace — it was okay to run now. The sooner the diamonds were out of his hands and inside the hotel, the better.

He sprinted down the East Drive path toward the obelisk, which rose from the trees in the distance. Even though it was dark he could see the park lights glinting off the granite monument.

As he got closer, he could see Isabel waiting for him by the base of the obelisk. She had her back to him, but she was unmistakable in her wool coat and skinny jeans, with a black hat pulled over her hair.

Ryan ran up to her, his breath releasing icy clouds into the frosty night air. He took the pouch with the earrings out of his pocket and slipped it into Isabel's gloved hand.

"I did it," he said proudly.

Isabel turned to him and smiled. "Thanks, Ryan!" she said, and Ryan gasped. It wasn't Isabel at all. It was Erin, from the Jewels!

Chapter Sixteen

Erin caught the stunned look in Ryan's eyes as he stood frozen for a second, not sure how to react. She knew she probably shouldn't have revealed herself to him, but doing that was too hard to resist. And it was worth it. The look on his face was priceless.

She savored the last moment, then quickly ran off. A few seconds later she heard Ryan's footsteps behind her. If he caught up, she'd be regretting her decision for sure.

Because of the map they'd found, the Jewels knew that Isabel was supposed to hand off the diamond to Veronica at the *Alice in Wonderland* statue. So the Jewels had mapped out their own route. Erin made a right-hand turn and began to run west across the park. After about a hundred yards, she spotted Willow waiting for her.

Erin slipped the velvet pouch into Willow's hand and her friend sprinted off without a word. The fastest runner on the quiz bowl team, she would be hard to catch, the Jewels knew.

Ryan caught up to Erin a few seconds later, puffing and panting. He glared at Erin, then took out his cell phone.

"Aaron, the Jewels have the diamonds! Willow is heading west on the Seventy-ninth Street transverse. You've got to intercept her."

Erin could hear Aaron reply something, and then Ryan frowned. "What do you mean, you're at the zoo? That wasn't the plan!"

Way to go, Eli, Erin thought. *You did it!*

Ryan's face was red with anger now, and Erin figured she'd better leave the scene. Besides, Ms. Keatley was sure to be missing her from the party by now.

Erin dashed after Willow, but she was nowhere near as fast. At the end of the transverse road she made a left. She could see Willow's red winter hat as she wove through the pedestrians on the path up ahead.

Finally, the white twinkling lights of the quiz bowl party came into view. As Erin got closer, she could see Willow, Jasmine, and Lili talking to Ms. Keatley. Jasmine and Lili had stayed behind to make it look like the Jewels were at the party. But Ms. Keatley's face was stricken with concern.

Erin ran up to the group as quickly as she could.

"Erin! There you are!" Ms. Keatley said with relief in her voice.

"Sorry, Ms. Keatley," Erin said, catching her breath. "I was just, um, uh . . ."

"Looking for the bathroom, like we told you," Lili finished for her. "It's, like, you think there'd be a bathroom around here, right?"

"Yeah, right," Erin said. "And I, um, I really had to go."

Ms. Keatley shook her head. "Next time, please let me know. I was about to send out a search party for you. I don't want you girls running off, okay?"

Willow and Erin exchanged guilty glances.

"Of course," Erin said. "Sorry."

Suddenly, Ryan ran up behind her, nearly knocking her over.

"Ryan! My goodness! Are you okay?" Ms. Keatley asked.

Erin felt a twinge of fear in her stomach. Would Ryan tell Ms. Keatley what had happened?

"Definitely not!" Ryan replied. "It's Erin! She . . . she . . ."

His voice faded as he realized that he couldn't tell the truth.

Of course, Erin thought. *He can't say anything without making himself look guilty, too.*

"I was giving him a hard time about how we're going to beat the Rivals tomorrow," Erin said quickly.

"Erin! That's very poor sportsmanship," Ms. Keatley scolded.

Erin hung her head in mock remorse. "I know." Then she turned to Ryan and flashed a triumphant smile, one Ms. Keatley couldn't see. "Sorry about that, Ryan."

He glared at her. "You're the ones who will be sorry."

"I don't like the tone of this conversation at all," Ms. Keatley said firmly. "Quiz bowl is competitive, yes, but ultimately it's about having fun and improving one's mind. This isn't *football*." Her voice dripped with disgust as she said the word.

Mr. Haverford strolled over, followed by Isabel, Veronica, and Aaron. Isabel and Aaron looked angry and sweaty, while Veronica mostly looked bored and cold.

"Is everything okay here?" he asked. Then he nodded to Ms. Keatley. "I see you've found Erin."

"Yes, apparently she and Ryan were getting into it about the quiz bowl match tomorrow," the teacher replied. "I apologize if anyone on our team is acting out of line. I'm trying to teach the girls to be good competitors."

"Oh, you know, that's part of the fun," Mr. Haverford said with an easy smile. "I'm sure there are no hard feelings. Right, Ryan?"

Ryan only glared in response.

"Okay, then," the advisor said amiably.

Around them, workers began to remove the party lights, and the vendors started to wheel their carts away.

"We should be getting back to the hotel," Ms. Keatley said. "We all need a good night's sleep for the finals tomorrow."

"Good idea," Mr. Haverford agreed. "And whatever happens tomorrow, I'm sure we'll all still be friends, right?"

There was an uneasy silence as the Rivals and Jewels stared at each other.

"Of course," Ms. Keatley said brightly, trying to break the tension. "And may the best team win."

Erin grinned. "We already have," she said, looking right at Ryan.

Chapter Seventeen

"**We** did it!" Erin shrieked, jumping up and down on the bed. "Go, Jewels!"

"Goooooo, Jewels!" Willow, Jasmine, and Lili cheered.

All four girls collapsed on the bed in giggles. It was still so hard to believe. Their plan had worked!

"Tell me again how Ryan's face looked when he realized he gave the diamond to you?" Jasmine asked with a dreamy look on her face. "I wish I had a picture."

Erin grinned. "He was totally shocked. It was awesome," she replied. "I never thought I'd say this, but I guess it's a good thing I'm sort of the same height and shape as Isabel. He didn't suspect me for one second. Just handed the diamonds right over."

"Still, we're lucky he didn't stop you right there," Willow said. "The plan was to get the diamonds and run, to buy us some time."

"You know that nobody can catch up to you," Erin said. "Besides, Eli's really the one who saved us with his tech powers. After Ryan realized he'd been tricked, he called Aaron right away and told him to intercept you. When he found out that Aaron was at the zoo instead of Strawberry Fields, he turned bright red. So thanks for getting Eli to help us, Lili."

Lili shook her head. "Honestly, I know my brother's smart, but I never knew he was such a genius," she said. "Just think of what he could do with these powers of his."

"So, he actually hacked into Ryan's phone?" Jasmine asked.

"No," Willow replied. "He was able to send text messages to Isabel, Aaron, and Veronica, making it *look* like they were coming from Ryan."

Jasmine shook her head. "All the way from Hallytown. Amazing."

"And those guys bought it," Erin said. "Eli told them that their coordinates had changed, and he sent them to different areas of the park — and out of Willow's way. Beautiful."

Lili grinned excitedly. "Tonight, they lost, and we finally won!"

"Ooh, can we see the diamond earrings, please?" Jasmine asked, lowering her voice.

Willow nodded. "If we read that diary right, then one of these diamonds is a clue. Maybe you can find something, Jasmine."

The girls sat cross-legged on the bed in a circle as Willow produced the pouch and gently placed the two earrings in Jasmine's hand.

"They're beautiful," Jasmine whispered, her eyes growing wide. "I wish I had a jeweler's loupe or something, so I could get a better look."

Erin jumped off the bed. "I've been carrying this around ever since we started this detecting stuff." She rummaged through her overnight bag and pulled out a large magnifying glass. "It helped us figure out that the Rivals stole the ruby, remember?"

"That could work," Jasmine said, taking it from her.

"You know, maybe we all need detective tool cases," Lili said with that faraway look she got in her eyes when she was creating something in her head. "They could be red — no, maybe black — with the letter J picked out in fake rubies."

"That's actually not a bad idea," Willow agreed. "It's good to be prepared. I'll start making a list of what we could put in them."

Jasmine held the magnifying glass up to her hazel eye, making it seem huge through the lens.

"You look like a cyclops," Erin joked.

"Shhh," Jasmine said, as her face screwed up in a look of total concentration. She brushed a strand of frizzy hair from her face and examined the two earrings one at a time.

"What do you see?" Erin asked impatiently. "Are there any clues?"

Jasmine didn't answer for a moment. Then she put down the magnifying glass.

"It's interesting," she said. "The diamonds are the same weight, but they're cut differently. Normally, the diamonds in a pair of earrings would be cut the same."

"What do you mean?" Lili asked, looking over Jasmine's shoulder.

"Well, see the little flat surfaces all over each diamond?" Jasmine asked, and Lili nodded. "Those are called facets. This one diamond looks like it's a rose cut diamond, because the facets are larger and there aren't as many. That was a popular cut in Martha Washington's time. But this other one looks like a brilliant kind."

Lili squinted. "Oh, yeah, there's a lot more facets, right?"

"Right," Jasmine said. "Brilliant cut basically means that the diamond has a lot more facets so it's more sparkly."

Willow looked excited. "So if the diamonds don't match, that means that one of them was replaced."

"By Martha Washington herself," Erin added. "One of these must be the special diamond. The clue."

Jasmine sighed. "I don't know what she means by 'clue.' Unless maybe it's the name of the cut. Maybe the rose cut diamond means the clue is a rose garden or something."

Willow jotted that down in her notebook. "Could be. Are you sure you don't notice anything else?"

Jasmine studied the diamonds some more. "Well, the setting on the rose cut diamond is a little loose," she said.

"Can you get it out?" Erin asked eagerly.

Jasmine looked horrified. "But this is a priceless antique!"

"It's more than that," Erin pointed out. "It's part of a big mystery that we're caught up in."

"Erin's right," Willow agreed. "We're mixed up in something important. We went to a lot of trouble to get those earrings. We need to find that clue."

Jasmine sighed. "Does anyone have, like, tweezers or something?"

"I brought my beading kit with me," Lili answered. "I use my tweezers to pick up the tiny ones."

"You brought your beading kit with you?" Erin asked.

"You never know when you need to add a little sparkle to something," Lili replied. She handed the tweezers to Jasmine. "Here you go."

Jasmine sighed and put down the magnifying glass. She carefully began to pry open the tiny bars of silver holding the diamond in place.

"I hope I don't break anything," she muttered under her breath.

The girls were silent as Jasmine worked. Then a look of relief swept over her face.

"Got it," she said as the diamond popped out. She handed it to Willow, who picked up the magnifying glass. "Be careful with it, okay?"

Willow turned the diamond around in her fingers, examining it from every angle.

"Is there a clue? Is there a clue?" Erin asked eagerly.

"Oh my gosh, I think there is!" she said, her voice rising with excitement. "It looks like there's something etched on the back of the diamond." She moved the magnifying glass closer to it and then a little farther away, trying to get the best image.

"It looks like the letter E, and then the number fifty. See?" Willow gingerly handed the diamond back to Jasmine.

"Wow, you're right," Jasmine said, after examining it herself. "E fifty. But what does it mean?"

Willow quickly jotted it down in her notebook. "I have no idea," she said. "But it's definitely some kind of clue."

"A clue to what?" Erin asked. "And does this mean there's a clue on the ruby, too?"

"Probably," Willow reasoned. "If there's something etched on the back of the ruby, they've probably seen it. That is, if they even know about the clues. We only know about them because of the diary. Maybe the Rivals want the jewels for a whole other reason."

Erin held out her hand, and Willow passed her the diamond. Lili and Erin looked at the etching together.

"This is amazing," Erin said. "Things are definitely getting interesting."

Jasmine took the diamond back from her and put it in the pouch. She had a guilty look on her face.

"So what do we do with this now?" she asked. "I mean, we found the clue. But these earrings are stolen! Couldn't we get in trouble for keeping them?"

"I totally didn't think of that," Erin said. "But I guess you're right. I guess we could put them back in the desk."

Willow frowned. "But we don't have the key. And if we do that, the Rivals could always go back and get it."

"What if we just send them back to the museum, you know, anonymously," Jasmine suggested.

"That doesn't seem right," Lili piped up. "I mean, the museum didn't even know they existed. Nobody does. So how can we get in trouble for stealing something that didn't belong to anybody?"

"The diamond belonged to Martha Washington," Erin pointed out. "And we go to the school named after her. So maybe it makes sense if we keep them."

Jasmine rubbed the side of her nose, a sign that she was stressed or nervous. "I don't know, guys, it still feels wrong."

"I think we have to hold on to it," Willow argued. "We have to make sure the Rivals never get it. Just in case they *are* collecting clues."

"I just thought of something," Jasmine said. "The diary said it wasn't safe to keep the four clues together, right? So there must be clues on the sapphire and emerald, too. Maybe the Rivals have those two jewels, and maybe they don't. But as long as we have the diamond, we can keep safe whatever Martha Washington wanted to protect."

Erin nodded. "It's our duty to protect it. For Martha."

Lili held out her right hand. "For Martha!"

Willow put a hand on top of hers, and then Jasmine reluctantly did the same.

"For Martha!" the four Jewels vowed.

Chapter Eighteen

The next morning the girls couldn't stop smiling as they ate their breakfast.

"My goodness!" Ms. Keatley remarked. "Usually you're more serious before a match. You all look as if you've already won."

Erin swallowed the piece of bacon she was chewing before replying. "We're just excited to get started. After winning yesterday, we feel as if anything is possible today!"

Lili nodded, picking up on her teammate's meaning. "We're feeling kind of invincible!"

Ms. Keatley frowned. "Don't get overly confident. You've got to keep on your toes. Today are the finals. You'll be facing your toughest competition yet."

"We're ready," Willow said firmly as Jasmine nodded in agreement.

"Then let's go!" Ms. Keatley stood up and together they took the short walk back to the auditorium at Kane College.

They got there just as the other quiz bowl teams were streaming in. The atmosphere in the room was tenser than it was yesterday. A nervous, excited energy could be felt throughout the room. After all, one of the teams would be named the Quiz Bowl Regional Champion today.

The girls and Ms. Keatley found seats together. Just as they were sitting down, the Rivals entered the auditorium. Mr. Haverford spotted Ms. Keatley right away and eagerly walked over, with the reluctant Rivals trailing behind him.

"Good morning! Big day today," he said as he beamed at her.

"It certainly is," Ms. Keatley responded. "Good luck to your team. I know they've been working hard."

The moderator, an older woman with bright red hair, stepped onto the stage.

"Looks like we're getting started," Mr. Haverford said as Ms. Keatley opened up the program and started reading. "Maybe we could meet at the break for lunch?"

"What?" she asked, lifting her eyes off the page. "Oh, we'll see."

They left to find seats. Ryan glanced back at Willow. This time he didn't grin. He raised his chin and gave her a defiant look that said *no mercy*.

Fine, thought Willow. *It's on*.

The first round of the competition began. The Rivals were called to the stage and squared off against a team from Maryland.

For the first time in a match, the Rivals weren't at their best. In fact, they seemed flustered. They got a couple of questions wrong.

"Who is the god of the underworld and precious metals —" the moderator began. Aaron buzzed in before she finished the question.

"Hades," Aaron answered.

"Incorrect," she said. "The Atkinson Rivals will receive a penalty for interrupting the question with an incorrect answer."

She turned to the Maryland team. "Baltimore Brainiacs, this is your chance to answer. Who is the god of the underworld and precious metals in *Roman* mythology?"

A girl from the Brainiacs hit the buzzer. "Pluto?"

"Correct," the moderator answered.

Jasmine looked at Willow, her eyes wide. "The Rivals usually don't make those kinds of mistakes," she whispered.

"What happened yesterday must really be getting to them," Willow said. "Maybe they won't make it past the first round today!"

The Rivals struggled for a few more questions before requesting a thirty-second time-out, using the only one they were allowed in the game. They huddled together, then went back to their buzzers, looking serious.

Whatever was said during the time-out worked. The Rivals began wiping the floor with the Brainiacs, nailing question after question until they were victorious.

Jasmine sighed. "I guess they've got their mojo back."

Then it was the Jewels' turn. They were facing a team from Connecticut, the Stamford Smarties.

"I almost forgot!" Lili pulled the tiaras out of her bag before the girls took to the stage. "They brought us luck yesterday."

Erin stuck one on her head. "They did! Now for a team cheer!" she cried, and the girls formed a circle, wearing their tiaras.

"History!" Erin cried, putting her hand in the center of the circle.

"Math!" Willow yelled next, adding her hand.

Jasmine put hers on top of Willow's. "Science!"

Lili slapped down on Jasmine's. "Art!"

"Go, Jewels!" they cheered

They took their places on stage. The Smarties were tough, but after a fast-paced match, the Jewels managed to prevail.

The rest of the morning was a blur as the girls competed.

"0.1667!" "Symbiotic!" "Botticelli!" "Jackie Robinson!"

The Jewels were on fire as they got one answer after another right. They won their next two matches, then there was only one other team left to face: the Rivals.

"Why did it have to be the Rivals?" Erin wailed, before greedily gulping down some water during the break.

"We can do this," Willow said. "We've made it this far. There is no reason why we can't beat the Rivals in the finals."

Lili smiled. "Let's do it!"

They climbed back on the stage for the final match of the day to determine who would win the regional championship. The audience grew quiet as they entered the stage with the Rivals. The silence was eerie, and the girls began to feel more nervous than they had all day.

"Go, Jewels!" a loud shout broke the silence. It was George, their friend from the Allentown All-Stars.

"Yeah! Go, Jewels!" Lauren joined in. Soon others began clapping and cheering for the Jewels. The Rivals' reputation for nastiness had followed them to regionals. They hadn't made a lot of friends.

Isabel sniffed as she stood behind her buzzer, pouting at the crowd's enthusiasm for the Jewels. Veronica had a determined look on her face, as did Aaron. Ryan acted like he didn't care about the crowd. He wore the same smug smile he always did.

"Quiet, please!" the moderator silenced the crowd. "I'd like to welcome the Martha Washington Jewels and the Atkinson Prep Rivals to the final round of our tournament. Let's begin."

The crowd settled down as the moderator asked the first question.

"What three minerals make up granite?"

Willow glanced at Jasmine and gave her an encouraging smile. She knew her friend would get this one!

Jasmine buzzed in, seconds before Veronica did.

"Martha Washington," the moderator said.

"Feldspar, quartz, and mica," Jasmine answered.

"That is correct," the moderator replied.

The audience clapped enthusiastically. The Jewels were off to a great start! Because they got a question right, they got to answer a three-part bonus question, which they nailed. That gave them a forty-point lead right out of the gate.

"What name did American colonists give the series of laws passed by the British Parliament after the Boston Tea Party?" the moderator asked.

I got this! Erin thought as she hit the buzzer, beating Isabel to it.

"The Intolerable Acts," Erin answered confidently. She shot a snarky smile at Isabel, who rolled her eyes in response.

"Correct," the moderator said, once again to the cheers of the crowd.

Willow beat Ryan to the buzzer over a complicated math problem. Lili identified the art movement called Impressionism before Aaron could. The girls were doing great, but then the Rivals began to make a comeback.

Ryan answered a math problem first, flashing Willow his smug smile as he did. Aaron got an art history question right, and Veronica and Isabel both scored for the Rivals, too. The competition was heating up!

The questions kept flying and the buzzers were getting a serious workout as the two teams went head to head, battling it out for the title. In what seemed like the blink of an eye, time was up.

"The score is tied," the moderator said. "We need to go into a tie-breaker. Three tossup questions will now follow."

Willow gave a thumbs-up to her team. They were so close to beating the Rivals! Lili smiled cheerfully. Jasmine looked determined. And Erin's face was flushed from the excitement. But across the stage, Ryan was frowning. *They look worried*, Willow thought.

"According to the periodic table of the elements, what is the symbol and atomic number for calcium?" the moderator asked.

Veronica beat Jasmine to the buzzer by a fraction of a second.

"C-A-twenty," she answered.

"Correct," the moderator said.

Willow grew nervous. If the Rivals got this question right, it was game over!

"What is the name of the Swedish author who wrote *Pippi Longstocking*?"

Erin banged the buzzer so loud the slap echoed throughout the auditorium. "Astrid Lindgren!" she cried.

"Correct," the moderator confirmed as the crowd clapped.

The girls exchanged nervous glances. This was it. If they got this question right, they would be the champs!

"This Greek mathematician reinvented how pi was estimated. Name him or her."

Willow knew the answer! She pressed the button, but her heart sank as she heard the sound of a Rivals buzzer a split second before hers.

Across the stage, Ryan smiled smugly. "Archimedes."

"Correct!" the moderator cried. "And the winners of the Quiz Bowl Regional Tournament are the Atkinson Rivals. Congratulations!"

The crowd clapped politely, but some of the students who had previously lost to the Rivals groaned. Ryan slapped Aaron on the back as they grinned at each other. Isabel and Veronica hugged. They then crossed the stage to shake hands with the Jewels.

"I'm not going to lie, you had me nervous there for a little bit," Ryan said while shaking Willow's hand. "I think I may have underestimated you, in more ways than one."

He shot her a knowing look. They both knew he was talking about the diamond.

"But don't worry," he added. "It's a mistake I won't make again."

Willow gave him an icy smile. "You may have won regionals, but we're going to take nationals, you can count on it."

Just as the Rivals were leaving, Ms. Keatley came rushing onto the stage.

"Girls, I am so proud of you all!" she said. "You did an amazing job. Second place! It is quite an achievement."

Willow smiled. "I would have liked to have won, but you're right. We did great!"

"There is going to be an awards ceremony," Ms. Keatley said. "I need to fill out some paperwork first. I think you're getting a trophy! I'll be right back."

As Ms. Keatley walked away, Erin opened her arms wide.

"Group hug!" she cried.

They all grabbed each other. "We did awesome!" Jasmine said.

"Um, guys, I can't breathe," squeaked Lili, who was trapped in the center.

Laughing, they broke apart.

"We may not have won, but we've proven that we can stand up to the competition," Willow said. "I'm proud of us. And I think I spotted a pattern in the Rivals' incorrect answers. We can come up with a study strategy to cream them the next time we face off!"

"Whoa! Relax!" Erin held up her hand. "One quiz bowl tournament at a time."

Jasmine laughed. "Yeah, let's celebrate how great we did here first. But Willow is right. I feel more confident than ever."

Lili looked around to make sure no one was nearby. "And to think we stopped them from getting their hands on the diamond. It wasn't easy, but we did it!"

"It's not over," Erin reminded them. "If the Rivals really are collecting clues, they might try to steal the diamond back. And we need to find out if they have the emerald and the sapphire."

"We're the Jewels — we can do anything we put our minds to!" Lili cried as she held out her arm. Willow, Erin, and Jasmine each reached out and put a hand on top of hers.

"Gooooooo, Jewels!"

Help the
JEWELS
with the next heist!

Turn the page for a super secret sneak peek at the third book in the Jewel Society series!

*W*illow nodded at Lili. "I've been doing some research, too, to try and figure out what the E-Fifty on the back of the diamond could mean. It could be part of a math equation. Also, there is a World War Two tank that has a model number E-Fifty, as well as a smartphone. But those are way after Martha's time, so I ruled them out. I'm thinking the E-Fifty will make sense once we see the clues on the other jewels."

"*If* we see the clues on the other jewels," Jasmine pointed out. "The Rivals definitely have the ruby. For all we know, they might have already stolen the emerald and the sapphire, too."

Erin nudged Jasmine. "*Shhh!* Here comes Principal Frederickson!"

A stern-looking African American woman marched into the library. Principal Frederickson always walked like she knew exactly where she was going. Today, she was headed right for the girls' table.

The Jewels quickly stopped talking and closed their notebooks.

Erin greeted her in her most polite voice. "Hello, Principal Frederickson."

Their principal raised an eyebrow, and Erin swore she saw something resembling a twinkle in her eyes.

"You don't have to hide anything from me, girls," she said. She leaned forward, placing her hands on the table. "I know what you're doing. And I know all about the Martha Washington jewels."